MOMENT OF TRUTH

The Captain swiveled suddenly in his chair and Clay saw it—a nickel-plated Colt .44 like some tiny, beautiful, and deadly animal, sleeping in his hand.

"You see?" he said. "I have you."

They were close together, locked in that stone-walled house. They were good shots. Even their misses, broken to fragments on the walls, would become deadly ricochets. There was no way either of them would walk from that room untouched.

"Well . . ." the Captain shrugged nonchalantly. Some reflex in Clay was alerted. Clay knew it was the beginning of the man's move.

A sheer fraction of a second before his thumb hooked the hammer of that fancy Colt, Clay's hand swept up, and the gun in it was erupting with flame and thunder.

Other Blazing Western adventures from Dell Books

WIND STALKER

by

Owen G. Irons

A DELL BOOK

Published by
Dell Publishing Co., Inc.
1 Dag Hammarskjold Plaza
New York, New York 10017

Dell ® TM 681510, Dell Publishing Co., Inc.

ISBN: 0-440-19076-2

Printed in the United States of America

First printing—April 1980

ONE

Pa had gone, taking the black and his sheepskin, the Sharps .50, and a month's supply of grub. So I would be alone for a while, but it didn't worry me any. I had been alone on the ranch many times since we came north. Montana was my home now, the Milk River country my world. I had to stop and struggle to remember a time when we had not lived in the far north country where the winters were long and hard, the summers short but delicate and sweet, filled with the smell of flowers spread over the valleys and the surprised singing of birds in the long stands of pine.

I took out the fork and began pitching hay. I had time for maybe two hours' work, and I got to it. Pa expected it of me now, and I expected it of myself. I was sixteen and big for my age, broad in the shoulders from axing and pitching, dragging stone with the mule, pulling stumps, digging out the springs . . . all manner of work, all year round. My face was harder than my years too. I already had the Rourke lines to it and the dark blue eyes of all the men on my pa's side.

I had never seen any of the family. There had been some kind of trouble when Pa married my mother and left out of Oregon, but I had seen likenesses.

Pa had hated to go. I could see it in those blue eyes

of his. The same deep eyes I saw in my own reflection. And in the set of his wide mouth.

He and I had been close. We had to be. The nearest neighbors, not counting the Nez Perce I had seen camped on the Marias and the Gros Ventre up the Milk, were the Collinses, who were fifty miles away, toward Fort Walsh on the Canuck side of the line. Pa had seen the Big Bellies, the Gros Ventre too, and it worried him some. We had once had some trouble with a band of these Indians.

A small band under a warrior called Black Tooth had come trading and made off with our mule in the process. Pa found Black Tooth's men ready to roast the animal when he rode down on them and spoke to them a little with that old '62 Henry rifle. One of the first repeaters the Winchester company had pumped out, the old weatherbeaten Henry spoke with a harsh tongue. The Gros Ventre came around to Pa's way of thinking on that mule and cut him loose. Time to time we had some trouble with Black Tooth, and I knew Pa didn't like leaving me alone.

Thing was, why did he?

I thought on it careful and the only answer I came up with was the one that eventually proved to be the right one—he was afraid I'd be in more danger where he was headed.

The sky was paling with the coming grayness as I walked to the barn. Old Dewslip, our half-blind roan, had his ears pricked, watching the sky with a dislike. We hadn't yet had bad weather this autumn, but there was an odor in the air that Dewslip didn't like. He was old now, nearly thirteen, and he liked the sun on his back of the mornings and the high summer grass.

I took to pitching, throwing the cut hay into the

loft with an easy motion. I was sweating despite the coolness of the day, but I liked the rhythm of the work. After a time my muscles seemed to respond on their own, knowing what was expected of them and doing it. I had time to think.

"Clayborne," my pa had said as we sat across the table, a cup of coffee in his work-gnarled hands, his eyes sharp on me, "I've got to be going away for a time."

"Away?" The notion struck me funny right off. It was time to be laying up for winter. We had been cutting fuel wood for a week and planned on another week of it at least. Then we were going to finish the haying and patch up the roof.

"I don't want to . . ." he hesitated. "There's an opportunity that can't wait." He looked doubtful for a moment, his long face concentrating on what to say. "In Colorado."

"Colorado!" Lord, that was most a thousand miles of mountain travel. "I'll be alone for the winter."

"Yes, I know you will, Clay. That's what has made the decidin' so hard. But there's some business. With a man name of Hewitt. Hewitt," he repeated again as if telling me something. His voice was sort of far away. "But you're a strong boy, Clay. Once the snows come the Indians will be holed up too. You won't have any trouble with Black Tooth."

That was true. The Gros Ventre would not be hunting in the winter. Not hunting trouble. The long snows which covered the grasses made war impossible, or nearly so. Without graze for the horses the Gros Ventre would be holed up with their squaws, telling their tales, smoking, waiting out the long winter. But still I didn't like it. But I didn't question my pa. He would always do what he thought was for the best.

And he hadn't raised me to question his every decision.

"It'll be something grand for us, Clay," he said. The fire was low, and the shadows on his face caught the sorrowful hollows of his cheeks. "There's some money owed to me," he explained. "We can have us a real place. There's an almighty lot of grass up country where cattle could grow fat—if a man has cattle."

So far there were none that I knew of in the north country, only milk stock here and there. But the Texas cattle, prolific on their home graze, had been moving north slowly. In Kansas there were ten times the number of beef there had been the year before, with the railroad coming in. Into Nebraska and west, to New Mexico and even Arizona, the longhorns were being driven by men with ambition and grit.

Folks doubted the cows could winter in Montana, but Pa didn't. Not for a minute. He told me of winters in the Panhandle and up into the San Juans where cattle had survived brutal winters. "They're a tough breed," he had told me then. Now he had the opportunity to try it.

All of this was running again through my mind as I pitched hay. Suddenly I heard something low and afar off. A whistle like a magpie, but it was no magpie.

I held the pitchfork on my hip and worked to the door of the barn where my rifle lay against the plank wall. I stood softly in the shadows, smelling the dusty day outside. The sky had come in lower and the wind picked up. Grass and leaves drifted past, low to the ground. Then I saw old Dewslip. Lying dead next to the trough, his eyes wide to the sky.

The cool steel of the Henry had replaced the wooden shaft of the pitchfork. I cocked her down hard, the click sounding unnaturally loud, and stepped outside.

The house! There were black wreaths of smoke curling up from the roof and orange flame jutting out the door and windows. I dashed for it without thinking and heard a report, sawdust leaping at my feet. The smoke was boiling up, and I was pinned down behind the rain barrel.

I couldn't see who was shooting, but time to time I caught the smoke from a rifle up in the stand of lodgepole pines on the north ridge. I took a slow bead, aiming high for the distance and the rise and peppered the hillside with three or four shots. Then I turned and rolled toward the house. Already the siding was black, charred, the beams a-buckling.

I had my coat soaked from the rain barrel and I threw it over my head; staying low, I went in along the floor. I knew every inch of that cabin, and even with the smoke and the crackle of burning timbers, I found what I wanted quickly.

I stretched up my hand and took my pack from its hook. Overhead the roof was sagging, and she dropped in as I snatched my pack. The bag was canvas, smoldering, but I got it and broke into the outside again, moving as I did so.

And it was a good thing I had. I rolled to my feet and came face to face with a bearded white man. As I reached my feet he touched off the old rifle-musket he was carrying, the shot deafening in my ears. I threw myself to the ground and steadied to face him.

"Boy," he said wagging a big buffalo head, "I got to do you." He had an axe in his hands and he stood over me, blocking out the sun. Behind him heat waves from the cabin danced and wavered. I heard a horse blowing in the yard somewhere, and the light flashing on his axe blade stung my eyes. I didn't want to do it. I wouldn't have thought I could, but my finger had thoughts of its own. It twitched on the trigger of that Henry rifle for a moment, and as the axe swung down in a blur, it pulled. The man's face disappeared in a mask of blood.

Clutching his eyes, he toppled forward, swinging in a circle. He fell on top of me, blood streaming out. Again I heard a horse blow and heard hoofs approaching. It might have been help coming—but if so, where was it coming from? I never was to know. I only wanted to get out from there. The bearded man was lying on me. A big, bulky man, he must have gone two hundred and fifty pounds. He stunk, his dead eyes pressed close against my face. I jerked and shoved and then I was free. I had my satchel in my hand, the Henry in the other, and I took to the hills, running till my breath was gone, my chest knotted and shot through with fire. I was into the timber and far below I could see the cabin, only a sad, smoldering heap, the smoke trailing off across the grayish green of the country into the flat slate skies. I sat there and I shivered, my hands still tight on the rifle. And I knew already that I would never see my home again.

TWO

The snow that had been threatening began to fall.
Through the black thickness of the night, the slight,
early snowflakes drifted and collected on the wind
side of the pine, smothering fallen logs and exposed
ledges. Still, it was light, and soon would break and
melt.

I stayed close to my fire. Banked against the face of
a wedge between two giant, upright slabs of granite,
it was of necessity a small fire. I did not know who
would want to kill me, burn my house, destroy all my
pa had worked for, but I knew they wanted me dead.

At first I had thought of the Gros Ventre and Black
Tooth, but even before I had faced the big white
man, I had known it was not the work of Indians, although maybe it was supposed to appear that way.
Old Dewslip had been killed. I had never known an
Indian to kill a horse like that. Not except to eat. But
these men had killed our old roan.

I waited, the wind turning around me, whipping
through the upper boughs of the sheltering trees. I
waited and I watched, peering into the night, for I
knew they would come if they could.

I ate a little of the jerky I had packed in my pack
and mixed a little thin coffee, although I seldom
drank it. I also had my skinning knife in there, a

dozen fish hooks, and some other odds and ends like a fishing line, a magnifying glass, spare socks, and my compass. I used the pack for when I went exploring in the high up mountains, fishing the lonely, quick running streams. It wasn't always easy to predict when I would make it home, so Pa encouraged me early to carry a few necessities.

Pa . . . I thought again of his going, his long, serious face. What would I do now? I had no plan. He was on his way to Leadville, away down in Colorado. And before he reached it the high passes would be clogged with snow, the rivers frozen, the trees cold and naked. He would have to winter in a hotel or some other lodging. That meant I would not see him under any circumstances until spring. And I was of no mind to stick it out where I was, although I knew the country like my own homely face and loved it.

I waited, watching silently into the darkness. Nothing moved in all the world but the quick flying snow, the waving black treetops, the wind whistling in the crevices. At some point I fell asleep, the Henry cradled across my lap.

When I woke it was gray, the sun glittering through the frosty trees. The snow had not stuck much, and lay only in the shadows and low places where the sun had not yet reached. But it was cold and windy still. With a start I realized what had awakened me. Voices.

There was somebody moving around above me where the wedge of granite folded back onto a ledge. To where I was there was no sight line. A man would have to hang out in space to see past the clumps of brush. Quickly, I edged back into the darkest recess of the shelter, thankful that the fire had burned negligently out. There were three of them and I could hear them clearly in the still air.

"I can't see a blessed thing."

"Kid probably knows every rabbit run and squirrel hole in these hills," another man spat with disgust. I held still, not liking the tone of their voices.

"We'll root him out." This man had a high-pitched voice, slightly lisping. I thought I could recognize it again if ever I had the chance. "Captain wants this kid out of the way."

"I know what the Captain wants! Let him come up trekkin'. Goddamn, it's cold."

"We'll spread out. Jake, keep a watch here, will ya? You'll be able to see most of the valley. And if anything out there moves, shoot it!"

Jake was the one who had been muttering about the cold of the day. He sat down on the ledge not fifty feet above me. His feet knocked loose a few pebbles which actually hit me. I waited a moment. Not too long. If they were going to flush me, they'd have to circle back on the head rock and drop down into the ravines. It would be only a few minutes before they were again on open ground. Then I would be a treed coon. I waited, counting slowly to fifty.

"Hey!"

Jake jumped up as I ran from the shelter, the rocks rolling under my feet. He had been rubbing his hands together, leaving his rifle resting on a rock beside him. By the time he snatched it up and fired, I was behind a healthy-sized cedar down in the wash.

His bullet bit deeply into the tree, baring the white flesh under the ragged bark. I'll give him this—he could shoot. But he was alone. The other two were still up in the ravines, out of sight, although I could hear one of them crashing through the brush trying to get to where the fighting was.

I sifted through the cedars, staying low and moving quickly from trunk to trunk. Jake got off another shot, but it wasn't even close to me. I don't know what he saw or thought he saw. There was another, even wilder shot.

For a time I heard feet coming up behind me, the occasional thwacking of tree limbs snapping back into place, leaves and twigs crushing underfoot, but then they faded away.

From what I'd seen all of the men were big. Any one of them could probably have crushed me with one hand, but I was long and lean and used to climbing; more, I knew those hills like no man but the Indians and I took every gully and went down every shale slide, wound through the brambles and thickets of tangled chokecherry and wild raspberries until I'd spun a trail a cottontail would have trouble following.

I was about a mile from the house, still trailing south, when I found Pa.

He was mighty peaceful, but dead. I'd been afraid all along that he'd never made it past Jake and his crew. They'd been layin' for us. For Pa, and me, to cover their slimy tracks. I took a branch from a dead yellow pine and scratched a grave in the dark earth for my pa.

I stayed there under the trees where the Crown Creek ran quickly through the narrow cut, making bubbly sounds across the rocks before dropping off into Cedar Gorge. I sat quietly, just remembering what my pa had done for me, what he had meant to me, until the sun began to fizzle and slide down behind the jagged screen of the hills. Then I walked another mile and made dry camp on a high bluff where the wind whipped steady and I could keep sight of my back trail.

Afar off I saw a tiny fire. A little spot of warmth on the dark, undulating earth where three men who had murdered my daddy sat warming their blood-stained hands.

I would find them. I would remember those faces, those voices, and in time I would find them. When I did I would kill them for it. Did I hate them? Folks talk of hate, and the way they talk it seems to me that to hate you have to hate unreasonably. Hatred is an insane notion, a fearful thing.

No. I did not hate them, but they had killed a good man. A man with strong hands, a gentle face, who enjoyed giving.

Maybe Jake and his cutthroats would not regret their actions even as they lay a-dyin', but they would never take another good man's life.

I waited until it was full dark, watching that fire. A light snow had begun again, floating like feathers through the night. I watched and I waited, then I waited some more. It was three hours till light when I went down and forded the creek.

Crawling on my belly, I came on their camp when the sky was graying with early light. Two of them were still asleep, rolled tight in the cocoons of their blankets, and the other sat a sleepy watch, a tin cup of coffee poking out from under his blanket tent.

I had the Henry at my shoulder, sitting cross-legged behind a screen of brush. I touched off and the crack of the rifle broke the dawn, sending the cup flying. The man stood up and grabbed for his rifle and my second shot put him down, grabbing desperately at his leg.

"The kid!" Jake yelled.

"It can't be the kid. He's scared out of the country. It's Indians, I tell you."

I had rolled to one side then scurried down the draw to my left. Topping out a small rise, I fired again. The first shot was too quick, but the second caught Jake in the chest. He staggered back as if kicked by a mule. The man on the ground was rolling around and screaming fiercely, cussing, holding his leg to stop the blood which had soaked his pant leg.

The third fellow had gone to his belly, and on my second shot he opened up with a flurry of shots. I could see the smoke from his muzzle rise after each shot, then I felt something snatching at my shoulder.

In a second that turned into a biting pain, and I slumped back, the red stain creeping down across my shoulder.

Jake was dead, I thought. And the other was out of it. But now I was hurt and the third man was to his horse, driving uphill at a furious pace. I crawled into the brushy ravine, my shoulder burning. I guess I was into shock, because everything was slow and loud, clumsy as I moved.

I blinked to clear my eyes of what I thought was sweat; but it was blood, and I was aware then of a burn along my scalp. The horse was right above me, a strapping bay with a deep chest, glistening with sweat.

"Kid!"

I swung my head around. He was over me with his pistol coming up from out of the holster at the back of his belt. I didn't even think of it this time, I only moved. The space between us was filled with a cloud of black-powder smoke and from it a face came. It was a face with white eyes, sneering lips, and wearing a dirty yellow mustache. A dead face. He buckled at the knees and went down, his pistol discharging as he collapsed to the earth.

Then it was still. Dawn peered over the low hill rise, silhouetting the twigs of the underbrush, making massive phantoms of the scraggly, windblown cedar. There was nothing but the pain, the trickle of sweat, the pain . . . and the lingering odor of gunpowder. I lay on my back, watching the yellow ball of the sun climb into the brisk blue skies.

Then I saw nothing at all for a long while.

THREE

◄●►

I woke with the cold dew on me. I was soaked to the skin and scared. The shock had worn off and my shoulder hurt like a hammer-banging anvil. There was no moon, only the ghost of one, a black ball dangling over the trees just backlighted by the stars. I was on the hill still, and beside me was a greasy-looking, yellow-haired man in buckskins. Dead, he was. And I'd done it.

Since they had come down on me, I hadn't really been thinking. Just running and fighting with all the animal instincts in me. Now I could see the man's cold, waxy face in the starlight, and I *knew* that I had caused his death. It was a feeling I did not like.

Looking around, I saw the bay gelding the man had ridden, standing shuddering close by. When I went toward him, bracing myself on my rifle, he hobbled back a step. He was hurt, his right shoulder crippled some. I had done that, too, I suppose. I took up his reins and led him off with some vague idea of patching him up.

Then I heard it.

Down in the dead black valley where the three men had been camped, a whispering, scratchy noise. I stood, holding the bay's muzzle so he wouldn't blow, and listened again. Then I made it out. A voice.

"I'm hurtin'," the voice said, so low that I could barely make it out. There was an unhealthy whistle in the voice. I hesitated.

"What the hell," I told the horse. Leaning on it, I went down into the valley, picking my way over rocks and brush in the coal blackness of the chill evening.

"I'm hurt bad."

It was Jake, still flat on his back, his shirt a mass of scabbed blood. The blood trickled from his mouth and there was an unhealthy pinkish tinge to it.

"Kid?"

"I hear you, Jake." He looked up quickly, surprised that I had learned his name.

"You gonna help me?" he asked.

"I reckon. If I can. You're in bad shape."

"Don't I know it," he said with a sigh that rattled through his chest. His dark eyes went shut with the pain.

He was a heavy man, most of two hundred pounds anyway, and in my condition, with him being dead-weight as well, I could scarce move him. Somehow I got him propped up against his saddle, a blanket stuffed in behind him. He sat there, looking hound-eyed at me, his eyes unusually big. His black beard was fouled with dirt and blood and his legs quivered time to time. Me, I wasn't so sure I was in better shape.

"I'll spark a fire," I told him. He nodded back at me gratefully. He watched me quietly for a long time, blinking his eyes rapidly. There was perspiration on his forehead despite the chill.

"You got tagged too," he panted, lifting a feeble, pointing finger.

"Thanks to you fellows," I said, and I said it

roughly as I had every right to. He watched me, a sly smile spreading on his thick lips.

"You got salt, kid. I'll give you that. You brought it to us."

From a man like Pa I would've taken that complimentary. But from Jake it was only a bitter reminder of what had gone before. Nevertheless, I commenced to clean his wound.

"Bad?" he wanted to know.

"Never seen worse. 'Course I ain't seen many gunshot wounds."

"It's bad. I knowed it." His head rolled back heavily. I had his shirt off and was trying my best to clean out the hole. That .44 Henry slug had gone in real neat just below the collarbone on the left side, but where it come out there was a jagged hole like you could drive a surrey through. I compressed the bleeding some and bound it tight as possible.

"Was it daylight I could maybe find some herbs do you good," I told him.

"Indian cures. You wise to that medicine?"

"Some. Pa, he showed me some. We had a bad hurt Crow stay with us one winter."

"Crows're good ones," Jake said. "Never set eyes on a thievin' Crow. Kid . . ." he started to say something, but it was hard for him. I turned my back and stirred up the fire, making coffee with my truck and a pot left hanging on a tree limb by one of them.

"Kid . . ."

"I got to tend myself," I snapped. I peeled off my shirt and moved to the fire. I didn't want any latecoming apologies, dying regrets and such. Maybe the Lord places stock in such things, but me, I wasn't yet of a forgiving mind.

Jake watched me, his cup gripped loose in his

hands. Time to time he'd hoist it unsteady to his mouth. Suddenly, I wasn't so sure he was going to die, and I'm not sure if I was glad for it or not.

I wasn't hurt as bad as I thought. The bone had been plumb missed and even the amount of meat torn free of my shoulder was surprising little considering how close the man had been.

"You see Trollis?" Jake asked suddenly. I kept buttoning up my shirt.

"Which one's he?"

"Short fellah. Blond hair, mustache. That's his horse you got there."

"He won't be needing it."

"Oh?" Jake studied me differently for a minute, like he was seeing me for the first time. I know there wasn't much to see, just a big raw-boned kid, stretched out pretty good for my age. But he was a-lookin' at my eyes. I stared back, not afraid of him.

"You killed Free Wyler down at your place."

"So?"

"Nothing. I was just thinking how it worked out. Funny, you know. Four of us growed men taking you on. And you kill Wyler and Trollis . . . probably me too. Maybe it was just our time."

"You were just wrong."

"We been wrong before, kid. Never made no difference. Hell, me and Trollis rode the Missouri border near a year, taking what we wanted. Wyler, he was a Texan, had him a ranger to his credit before he was your age . . . it must've been our time. Funny . . ." his voice trailed off, but in a minute his head snapped up.

"Where's that Bolen!"

"Bolen? He the one with a high-pitched voice? He run out, I reckon. Ain't seen him."

"That would be Bolen. He's a runner, all right. Why the Captain . . ." again his voice broke off. I went to him.

"The Captain? Who is the Captain? You got to tell me, Jake. Who was it wanted to kill my pa? What for? He never hurt nobody that I recollect."

He didn't answer, but I didn't think he was blacked out or dead . . . yet. "Damnit, you got to tell me!" I had my rifle hoisted, butt end toward him.

"Or what?" he said, his eyes still closed. "Or what— you gonna kill me?" He chuckled softly, painfully. "I took the Captain's money for this. I never have switched rails on a man I worked for, and I won't now." One dark eye opened slowly, he saw the rifle butt over his head, poised, and he let his eyelid drop shut again. "You're a good kid," he muttered. "A good kid. Go find yourself a place to grow up. Get goin' and good luck."

Foolishly, I held the rifle hoisted another minute. Slowly, I let it drop to my side. I knew I wasn't going to do it. I couldn't hate even this killer any longer. But I would find out. One way or the other. I would come across this Captain. There must be something in my pa's past, something that I could trace back. I would find the man.

And when I did, he would not be a man I could not kill.

I threw a blanket over Jake's shoulders and scooted well back from the fire, aware that one of them was still prowling out there somewhere. Bolen . . . I wanted to remember that name too.

The fire burned low and went out. I did not light it again, but sat huddled, my back to a large stone. Later still, when I could not hear Jake's troubled breathing anymore and figured him to be dead, I heard his voice from the shadows. "Kid, I didn't do no shooting. I just showed 'em the way up here. That's all."

"You shot at me."

"Did I? You didn't think them shots were a bit wide, kid?"

Then he was silent again, and I thought back to Jake's shooting. After proving to me he was a marksman by taking a gash out of the tree I was sheltered behind, there had been a second and a third wild shot. Very wild.

"Thanks for telling me," I said. He didn't answer and I didn't have the heart to say it again.

When it was light I made the coffee over, but Jake was sliding out fast and couldn't drink it. I left it beside him with a couple sourdough rolls I had packed and went to bury the dead man. I couldn't see no man left to the wolves.

I first off looked through his pockets, hoping to find something on the Captain. There were two letters inside his coat, one of 'em old as the hills, the ink faded. Waddell also had on him a dozen new shiny eagles. I buried them with him, tucking the letters in my pockets. Truthfully, I couldn't make much out of them. I had gotten to printing and could do a fair job of ciphering that out, but the handwriting on those letters was beyond me. One of them, the older one, was wrote by a woman—of that I was fairly sure.

I had turned back to the camp when I had a prickly feeling crawl up my spine. On a notion I went to the ground, and crawling to the rise, I saw them.

Black Tooth himself, it was. And he was staring at the hillside where I lay while a couple of his men rifled our packs. There was another dozen Gros

Ventre sitting their ponies around the camp. One of 'em held something I could not make out at that distance high in the air and whooped.

Whether Jake was alive or dead, I couldn't tell. But they had left him sitting just where he was. Black Tooth and another Gros Ventre with rank feathers knotted in his hair argued about something, with Black Tooth pointing up the hillside, at my tracks, I reckon. But they did not come, perhaps knowing I was up there with that Henry repeater.

I waited another minute. Then Black Tooth and his men gathered into a circle, separating the booty they had come up with. I saw Black Tooth pick up Jake's rifle and he yelled something.

Then, while they were busy, I scooted on down that hill, tearing myself on the rocks. I got into the gullys and along the narrow streambeds, trying to lose my tracks. Then, when I had done the best I could, I got to higher ground for better sight.

It was then that I realized it for the first time. Really realized it. "Boy, you got big trouble," I told myself. I was fifty miles from the nearest white settlement I knew of, with Indians of uncertain disposition all around me, in a land where the cold came like it owned the earth and the winds blew like they were sent from a wrathful hell. I was just under seventeen years old, orphaned, wounded fairly bad with no idea of where I was going or how to get there.

It was the fall of 1868, Montana Territory.

FOUR

The snows held back another week. My first inclination had been to head south, toward Colorado, but that was plainly a foolish notion that time of the year. So I headed southwest from the Milk, trying to pick up the Marias and from there make my way down river to Fort Benton on the upper Missouri.

With my Henry I had no need to fret for food, but I had not enough cartridges to waste a single one. The second day I downed a mule deer and took the time to jerk the venison.

The plains were leaden, frost gray, and the geese came over in long, unending migrations. Each morning the grass was sharp with the freeze, the individual blades thousands of tiny daggers.

My shoulder still pained me badly. It was raw and stiff, especially in the morning. I wasn't making good time and began to wonder about making it at all.

The fourth day south I spotted a party of Crow. They drew their horses up around me as I crested a low rise. Then they just looked.

"Fort Benton?" one of them finally said. He was a tall brave in a white Hudson Bay blanket and buffalo robe, his parted hair and forehead painted vermillion for medicine. They were far north for Crow, and I knew they weren't looking for no buffalo.

"Benton, yes. My father is the colonel there. He is waiting for me." I lied, not sure about these men.

"Benton," their leader said, then he broke off into Crow tongue. As far as I knew no Crow in Montana had ever harmed a white man; but these braves were surely hunting someone, and I'd hoped my story would cause some second thoughts if they had taken a notion.

"Have you seen Crow? More Crow?" He pointed north with his lance and I shook my head. Then after a minute's dispute they rode out silently. I was glad to see them go. Their leader was riding an Appaloosa—a Nez Perce horse—and a couple of the men had fresh scalps woven into their horse manes. I moved out quick, watching over my shoulder.

There was constant warfare between the Indian nations in Montana. Crow, Nez Perce, Gros Ventre, Blackfoot, and half a dozen others all raiding each other and collecting the scalps they needed for their braggin' tales. Pa and I had never had trouble with any of 'em, excepting Black Tooth. Maybe the Crow who had wintered with us that time had spoken well of us, I don't know. I knew only that it was no time to start having troubles.

I knew also that traveling alone, it would be an almighty stroke of luck not to have some.

I was camped along the Belly River, my fire set back in a rocky hollow where the lifting smoke was dissipated by the trees hanging low overhead. I was roasting the legs of four big bullfrogs I had gigged when I heard them coming.

There were six horses driving upstream, jets of water rising from their hooves. It was Black Tooth and he already had his gun out.

I was into the brush in a second, but too slow.

A brave came up beside me, rising like a jack-in-the-box out of the brush. I took my rifle and swung, catching the side of his head. He went down and I dove over him, a flurry of bullets following.

Where I was there was sheer rock facing the river with just a ribbon of sandy gravel, partly covered by brush. I was on the sand and running, horses behind me. I felt gravel kick at my legs and heard the echo of rifle fire twisting through the canyon cut.

"You're a dead boy, Rourke," I said. I lifted my rifle, spun around, and went to a knee just as a brave rode past me. I touched off and took the belly out of his pony. He tumbled over me, the horse sprawling.

Then he was to his feet, knife showing bright in his hand. The others were coming fast. I shot right into him and he spun around, blood leaking from his shoulder, but it wasn't a dead shot and he leaped at me, ready for the kill. He took the barrel and wrenched it from me.

I still had my hands on it. I could see Black Tooth a-comin', and hear him yelling. "Kill the boy!"

Using all the strength I could muster, the Indian still fighting me for the Henry, I got swung around and managed to get off a shot which somehow creased Black Tooth, sending him out of his saddle blanket. Then that Indian I was wrestling back heeled me and pulled back, my Henry in his hands.

He was running blood bad from his arm and he was mad. He took that Henry of mine to his shoulder and sighted.

Of a sudden Black Tooth's pony ran between us, and I took it by the mane with all the strength I had left. It dragged me for three running strides, and then I was on its back and riding free through the dark river bottom, the willows whipping past over the face of a pale rising moon.

After an hour I started to walk the pony. I hated to see that Henry go, but I guess it wasn't a bad trade for the horse. The only thing that had saved me was the Gros Ventre had never seen a repeater before, being used to muzzle loaders, and didn't know how to lever in a cartridge.

But I had me a horse, and I was breathing still. But I hated leaving those frog legs.

Five miles downstream I found me a good spot. High on a bench over the water, there was a little cut out from when the water had been higher. Scarcely visible behind a screen of brush, I had only happened to glance up and spot it while the moon was full on it. I picketed the white pony and climbed up to the cave. It was perfect. Only thing was, it was already occupied.

I heard the voices before I saw them, but as I started to back away from the cave, they came up out of the bushes behind me and a big hand was slapped over my mouth. I felt something sharp, hard, and angry at my ribs and I went limp. I wasn't arguing with no knife.

The cave was low roofed, glowing by the light of a small fire. Half a dozen Indians sat around it.

"Sit," one of them said.

"Obliged." I squatted beside the fire and they looked at me time to time.

"Eat, boy," their leader said again. I didn't have to be told twice. I cut myself a slice of that venison they had on the spit.

These were Bow-Piegan Indians, and there were six men traveling alone far south of their range. Remembering the Crows I had seen earlier, I figured something was up.

"You are from Banks-that-fell-on-them?" the old Indian asked me.

"No. From the Milk River. Pa Ka Eywa, you say?"

"Pa Ka Eywa." The old Piegan smiled faintly. "I have fished there often."

"You are traveling far," I suggested. I glanced at the others as I ate. Two of them seemed to resent my presence. One, a tall, very scarred warrior of thirty or so, glared back angrily as I spoke.

"You too." The younger brave interrupted angrily with a spurt of Piegan I couldn't pick up, but didn't have to. He wanted me gone. Or worse.

"Be silent, Orla Pola!" The older man waved a hand and the brave got up and skulked from the cave, his companion with him. The other Piegan were amiable or simply wooden.

"Orla Pola—Yellow Glove—he is a young man with fire in his veins. We are all tired . . . have you seen Crows?"

"One party. Not many men. Six. Seven. But it seemed they were looking for other Crow," I told him.

"Yes. Yes," the old man said heavily. His name, he told me, was Wind in Trees. Three weeks earlier a band of young Crow warriors had ridden down on the women at their washing and taken away three of them. One was Wind in Tree's daughter and Yellow Glove's wife-to-be.

"The warriors I saw were older men. Perhaps the raiders were renegades to their own people. Hot heads, wishing to count coup. These others may be hunting them."

"I think so," Wind in Trees agreed. "But it will

not matter. Yellow Glove must kill the Crow that took his woman."

We talked awhile longer. I explained about Black Tooth and at that the other braves' interest perked up some. Tales of battle were something they understood and respected. I didn't embellish it any, but told it just as it happened. That, too, they respected.

"A boy! He lies," a voice scoffed. I turned around to see Yellow Glove at the cave entrance. He appeared tense, inordinately so. Not that I could blame him, but he seemed to want trouble—any kind—as soon as he could stir it up.

"I don't lie." I said it softly, looking at Wind in Trees as I did so. "There is a white pony tied in the brush by the river. On it there is the mark of the Gros Ventre."

I rode with them at the dawning. I had no place else to go.

Yellow Glove didn't like a bit of it, nor did his friend, Quail Walker, but the others had granted me a grudging respect and treated me all right. Polecat, a one-eyed brave, and I became friends, as much as any white and red at that time could be. We shared a blanket and what food we snared or shot.

We rode steadily eastward, out onto the plains where nothing seemed to stir but the wind in the grass. The waterholes were churned to cold mud by a great herd of buffalo that had passed months ago. We were forced to dig for our water in the sinks.

On the seventh day we drew up on a low, yellow, grassed bluff. Polecat saw them first and he indicated them with a wave of his hand. We halted, the wind whipping our hair. Away off a tiny swirling stream of white smoke rose against a backdrop of dense alder.

"I think six warriors."

"And three of our women," Yellow Glove snapped.

"Crow!" Quail Walker spat angrily at the ground. In his hand, his sawed-off musket trembled.

"They will see us," Wind in Trees grunted.

"Let them see us. Let them see death as it rides down on them," Yellow Glove shouted, turning slightly in his saddle to see who was with him.

"We will see too much of it as well. It is a bad bargain," Polecat counseled.

"I'll go down." I said it suddenly. I don't know what made me say it, except these men, some of them, had become my friends in the few days I had ridden with them and shared their fire. I wanted to help.

"You?" Yellow Glove snorted derisively. "And what would you do!"

Quail Walker shook his head and spat again, the wind twisting his feathers over his face. I shrugged. "They won't know me. Why would they kill a white man who wouldn't even realize these squaws are not their own."

I paused, letting that work in their minds. Polecat nodded his head and turned his good eye toward Wind in Trees.

"It is true. They would not kill a white boy. No Crow would do that. They would suspect nothing of him."

"And then what would you do?" Yellow Glove wanted to know.

"I'll find a way. Loose the horses, maybe. Or kick their powder into the fire. Anyway, I'd be there, inside the camp."

"Take my gun," Wind in Trees said. The old man held out his prized weapon, a rifle-musket sawed off for easy use against the buffalo from horseback, decorated with brass studs in the stock, wrapped with rawhide where he gripped the barrel. It was a great show of faith.

"No," I told him. "I can't. They'd know it was not my weapon. Let them see me unarmed."

"We waste time," Yellow Glove decided. He sat his pony rigidly, his thick bronzed arms taut with determination.

"I don't wish to waste lives," Wind in Trees said, settling it.

"Send the boy! After he is killed we will do the work we came to do."

I slipped back onto my pony's back, and with the wind urging me down the long slopes, I rode out. I figured the encampment below had spotted me after I'd gone an easy half mile. They'd be keeping a sharp lookout, and there was a jumble of cracked grayish boulders just beyond the camp where I thought I'd seen a flash of sunlight on bright metal.

Still, there was no sign of movement in the camp. It was an eerie feeling. I rode that white horse easy along the sandy river bottom, tall alders and some cottonwood swaying in the breeze, changing green and silver as they turned their leaves. The pony's hoofs whished easily in the sand, the water ran shallow, in easy slow bends.

I could smell the smoke from the fire plain, and I heard a horse. I knew I was hanging it out. If these renegade Crow did decide to kill me, Wind in Trees was a good mile and a half back. I didn't dare glance back or give any indication that I was more than a wandering white kid.

Of a sudden I saw a quick shadow and thought I heard muffled sounds off to the south, behind the trees. If there were more of them behind that screen of alder, Wind in Trees and his Piegan would be caught in a well-designed trap.

As would I.

But there was nothing for it, so I rode ahead until I came to the clearing where the Indians had their camp. It didn't take me more'n a second glance to see I had ridden into big trouble.

"Welcome," the big brave laughed. I sat my horse just looking at him, my heart picked up to two beats for one.

"Step down," the Indian said. "I'll take the pony."

I looked at him, then once at the rifle he had on me and I stepped down easy. The Crow laughed out loud.

But it wasn't no Crow . . . it was Black Tooth.

FIVE

—————◆————————

I sat almighty still. The breeze, rising as the sun withered away, was cold off the north. The Gros Ventre were armed well. And at least one of them had a nice Henry repeater. The Piegans would be following me into camp soon, as the shadows gathered to conceal their movements; but it looked like they didn't stand a chance. There was nothing I could do about it. Nothing at all.

Black Tooth's men had tied me up, using a new elkskin rope and a good set of knots. My wrists were strapped behind me and to my ankles, and I was kneeling that way, hoping for Wind in Trees, half afraid to see him.

"At least you treated my pony well," Black Tooth told me. He smiled and patted my head roughly. I knew he would kill me. I suppose they had been anxious to kill me before because they thought I had seen something. Well, I hadn't, but I was seeing it now.

There were about a dozen of the Gros Ventre all together, and four or five of them were making up around the cooking fire. Making up to be Crow.

They took their hair and parted it, starting at the temple going up to the scalp lock, staining a part of the hair crimson along their foreheads. The Crow

I had seen the other day had done it the same way, cropping their hair in the middle so it stood up in a crest.

"Did you think the Crow would kill you?"

I looked around. It was a pock-faced Gros Ventre made up to be the spitting image of a Crow warrior. He got him a good laugh out of it.

They had them some Crow outfittings and they put them on for good measure—medicine bags tied into the manes of their ponies, ponies marked with Crow sign, leggings and robes—it was no mystery how they had gotten them.

My mind was in a tangle, still trying to figure out what I could do to warn Wind in Trees and the Piegan when I suddenly saw the squaws.

Two of them were older women, with the fat of some winters on them. The other, with big black eyes and a frightened smile, didn't seem to be no more than twelve years old or so.

They were tied together, backs to backs so that even if they wanted to run off it was physically impossible. The little girl looked at me, her eyes frightened, surprised, and I thought a little sorrowful for me. I smiled back, but it couldn't have been much of a smile.

I couldn't guess which of the older ones might have been Yellow Glove's future bride, but there wasn't much to choose between them. They weren't what you'd call unnaturally beautiful to begin with and had been dragged across country, with no chance to wash, probably little to eat, and treated some rough, by the bruise on the shorter one's cheek; but I guess there's no explaining taste. I knew some men who liked them plump for the shade in the summer, the warmth in the winter as they say; others appeared to like the ones that couldn't cast no shadow at all.

I just felt sorry for the three of them, especially the little girl. In a few minutes they would see their men fight and die. The sun was beginning to bleed out across the soft, high clouds. The sky, already silver and pink, was washing to a deep maroon near the rolling horizon. Shadows stained the earth darker hues in the canyon mouths and along the bottom land. The alders, along the river, were candlelit in their higher reaches with the last glinting rays of the vanishing sun.

They would come soon or not at all.

Then the crickets along the stream stopped their chorus of chirping. Black Tooth's head snapped up and he motioned with his hand. "Keep the prisoners together."

A rough-looking brave picked me up almost bodily and shoved me beside the women. Black Tooth snatched up the Henry rifle and levered home a cartridge. A covey of quail broke suddenly from the underbrush, their stubby wings whirring loudly.

I never heard a horse or footsteps, but they suddenly burst into the clearing. Wind in Trees was the first I saw, and he fired with his musket, a black cloud of smoke rising from it. One of the Gros Ventre caught the charge; his stomach slashed open, he flew backward with a ferocious scream.

Black Tooth was with the horses, and he laid down a screen of fire with the Henry repeater. One Piegan went down with a grunt and dragged himself off into the brush, leaving his musket. Black powder filled the campsite, the musket fire booming like never-ending thunder.

I saw Yellow Glove wielding a lance for a split

second. Then he disappeared in the confusion. In the near darkness the warriors moved like ghosts, dark shadows appearing, disappearing, all bloody, dust covered, and vengeful.

Down near me there was a Gros Ventre, bleeding horribly from the throat. And in his belt was a trade knife. I scooted to him, a musketball slapping into the tree beside me. Twisting around, I managed to get my hands on it and slash the elkskin rope free.

Then I was to the women, and as I freed them they darted into the shadows. But the girl was badly frightened, standing stock still.

"Run!" I told her. I grabbed an unloaded musket and took the girl by her wrist. "Come on!"

She made to break from me, but I took her away by main force. As we made our dash into the willow brush, I saw Black Tooth's glance pick us up.

"Get down!"

I had to push her, but it was a good thing I did. A bullet from the Gros Ventre's rifle whined overhead, ticking off a slab of yellow granite. Then I had the girl up again, weaving through the brush, the thorns cutting at us, the darkness closing fast.

I found a deer hollow deep in a thicket, and I pushed her into it. "They will need help," I said. I was panting, sweating cold in the night. The girl's eyes were wide, black, with no fear in them now. She did not understand but she made no move to get away.

"There may be other Gros Ventre over there." I motioned with my musket. Gros Ventre she understood and her eyes followed my signal. She nodded.

I hadn't forgotten the sign I had seen behind the alders, and if the Gros Ventre had heard the shooting, they would be into the camp by now. I had no idea what I could do. My musket was dry and I had neither ball nor powder, but maybe there was something . . .

I circled low into the riverbed. The gravel was warm beneath my feet, the water still in the shallow stream. I heard nothing. Not a single shot.

Crawling from the river, I came up at a point near where I thought Wind in Trees's Piegans had first entered the camp of the Gros Ventre.

It was dark now, cooling fast, the first high stars creeping out. I moved warily along the rabbit run. Here and there was a broken twig, grass trampled down, but I saw nothing else.

Then my hand went down on something warm, wet, and rubbery. With a grunt Black Tooth came out of the ground, his eyes astonished and furious. Frantically, I reached out, clawing at his face. His knife flashed and fell and I felt its bite low on my back.

I brought my knee up and he groaned as the wind went out of him. He backed away, knees wobbly. I could see he was hurt.

"You are bad luck to me, boy. I should have killed you long before. I should have burned down your father's lodge when I first saw him building it with his white hands."

He was weaving badly, but there was strength enough in him to do me. He had the knife low, blade up. He circled in as I got to my knees, groping for the musket.

"Stand away, Black Tooth." I pointed the short musket at him. "I'll kill you." Blood was filling my pant leg and I could feel myself going. The stars kept flashing in my head and it was unnaturally still, but for the buzzing which got louder and louder like a swarm of cicadas in my brain.

He laughed. A terrible laugh, long and rolling. "Empty guns do not kill," he said through his broken teeth. "And your gun is an empty one."

He stepped forward and I backed away. Something hit the backs of my legs and I fell backward over a rotten log. I remember his face flashing in front of me, the starlit sky far away, the cool grass coming to meet me. Instinctively, I pulled the trigger as he dove at me.

A gunshot tore open the night stillness, fire and rolling black smoke appeared and died slowly away. Black Tooth's mouth opened and blood began to run from it. I glanced at my musket and knew I had not done it.

Black Tooth staggered forward crazily, then lunged, falling beside me. I blinked hard, trying to focus, but I kept going out. The last thing I saw before the blackness cut out everything else was a tall Indian, painted for a Crow, standing over us, narrow slits for eyes, rifle still curling smoke.

SIX

◆━●━◆

I could smell wood smoke, see it twisting fine in the soft morning air. Somebody was cooking something, and I lifted my head to see the girl kneeling by me, and beyond her the two squaws hunched over the fire. My head hurt like nothing before and I let it fall back.

"Rest," the girl said. She touched a cloth to my head and I smiled. She shook her head worriedly and did not smile.

"So. You are back from the land of the dead." Wind in Trees was standing over me, my Henry rifle in his hands. "I have brought this back for you," he said, handing me the weapon.

"Thank you." I still couldn't puzzle out what had happened, but we were all right. The girl lifted my head a little and gave me to drink. It was sycamore tea, reddish colored, thin, but refreshing.

"My daughter is a fine nurse." Wind in Trees said it with pride. It took a minute to click.

"Your daughter?" If she was his daughter, this was the girl Yellow Glove would marry. This slight, big-eyed child.

"Wind on the Waters is her name. She is a good daughter to me." The old man didn't reach out for her but you could see his eyes, the pride in them go out and embrace her. I closed my eyes, letting the tea warm me.

"The Crow?" I blinked and rolled my head. There was a Crow standing right beside me. But not one of the Gros Ventre made up. It was the Crow I had met on the trail a week earlier.

"Shall I tell them at Fort Benton you are coming?" the Crow asked with the faintest of smiles.

"You're from there," I said. I should have known it. There was a contingent of Crow scouts at the fort, or so I had been told.

"Yes. But when we heard of the reports of Crow warriors raiding along the Marias, we came to see." He was a tall man, with two fingers missing. Not young any longer, but leathery tough. "These men have stained our reputation. The whites thought them Crows. Dressed as they were, what else could they think? But we knew they were not, and so we came to see who had taken our name."

"It was you behind the alders?"

"Yes. We were waiting the proper time. But when the Piegan came in, attacking, we came as well. These Gros Ventre will not shame the Crow—or their own people any longer."

"Let the boy rest now," Polecat suggested. He leaned over and touched my forehead. Then he opened up the wrapping on my leg and looked at it, grunting with satisfaction. "Your daughter does well," he told Wind in Trees.

"I'll walk?" I asked. My eyes were closed now. The sun was bright coming over the treetops. The earth beneath my back was warming.

"Walk!" Polecat laughed. "Yes, and run! Leap with the spring of youth. Clamber and stalk game. You will be fine."

He said something else, but I didn't hear him. I had gone off to sleep, dreaming of the hunt, a sparkling stream with the sun dancing in the cottonwoods, the high mountains beyond them.

I was on a travois when I awoke again, moving behind a pony ridden by Polecat. We were riding north and the sky was gray with coming weather, the wind hard off the north.

"So," Polecat said. "The lazy boy is awake again."

"Where . . . ?" The travois jolted over the terrain and my breath caught. I would be chasing deer all right, but no time soon.

"To the home of the Piegan. The winter will come soon. You cannot travel."

No, I couldn't travel. And the Piegan camp sounded like a fine place to winter. Come spring I would be sound and I would make my way south. There was still something to be taken care of. The Captain . . . I had not forgotten.

A man safe and snug in his home somewhere afar off had just opened his fat wallet and with that act he had taken my pa's life. While he sat smoking a cigar, feet propped up somewhere, my pa had dragged himself bleeding across the rocks, the scent of his own dying in his nostrils.

The girl appeared beside me, riding a gray pony with a black muzzle and tail. "Good morning, Wind on the Waters."

"She should not speak to you," Polecat told me. "Now she is not a small girl, but nearly a woman."

"She should know I am grateful," I replied, looking right at the little girl. She blushed and turned away, riding her pony in a prancing circle far out around the string of Piegan.

"Be careful," Polecat said to me. He said it in a

low voice. Then he turned back to his reins. The day was pleasant despite the coolness, and wrapped tight in buffalo robes I felt the chill only on my face. We glided easily across the long plains, stopping twice to water. I felt fine. But once a rider came up and I opened my eyes to catch the glittering eyes of Yellow Glove staring down at me, cold as ice.

"You are still alive?" he said sourly.

"And planning to stay that way." I had a grip on my Henry under the mound of robes.

"You are a friend of Wind in Trees. You will stay well. Unless there is an accident." His lips kind of twitched as if to smile, but instead he snapped his black pony with his quirt and swung off.

We made the Piegan camp three days later. There was snow on the ground; the trees were hanging with dripping water and slush. The whole camp—women with papooses and old men with long white hair—came out to greet us as we dragged in.

Wind in Trees explained briefly, about me. For a time there was a lot of fuss made over me. Some of the squaws wanted to rub their papooses to my breast, and the old ladies kept kissing me and bringing me drink.

They found me a place in a corner of the lodge shared by Polecat and his brother, his wife and kids.

"The children are curious too," Polecat said. "But in time they will grow accustomed to you."

There were three, two boys and a girl, all under five years old. For a while they stood back respectfully, and while I was wounded they left me alone. But soon they overcame their shyness, and as I healed they learned to know me, learned that I would accept their horseplay.

We spent the winter in the lodge quietly, happily.

The children crawled under my robes, clambered over me, grabbed at my hair and toes, wrestling, laughing, teaching me much about the Piegan tongue and about children.

"You encourage them too much," Polecat told me. At the time I was holding two of them under my arms while the girl, We Han, Small Dove, shrieked and clung to my neck.

"Yes," I admitted. "But a man who doesn't have the time to make a fool out of himself for children is a fool."

Polecat went away shaking his head, but his brother had heard the remark and he nodded at me. "Leave him alone, Polecat. They are all in love together."

It was in January when the snow had drifted ten feet high against the walls of the lodge. It was midnight, the sky hanging near and brilliant, clear. The drum talk began and after a while Polecat came to me.

"Get dressed." He said it softly, not to wake the children.

"Trouble?" I was already pulling my boots on, my Henry across my legs.

"No. No trouble. At the light we will hunt."

Food had grown short, I knew. One of the men had killed a winter-starved elk earlier in the week and we had enjoyed a chunk of the meat and the contents of the stomach—half digested grass which mixed with the natural acids tasted like a salad in vinegar and oil. But aside from that there had been little for a month. The jerked venison and buffalo meat was nearly gone, the maize low, and the occasional squirrels and rabbits too few and too little to sustain the tribe.

I dressed and was wrapped ~~in~~ my robe. Outside there was a fire crackling against the night. Too large for cooking or warmth, the giant bonfire snapped and threw off golden sparks. The snowbanks danced with light, and the men, their faces painted, chanted.

We danced like fiends around the fire all night until shortly before dawn. Great quantities of tobacco mixed with willow bark was smoked and wreaths of it hung in the air. At a signal from Wind in Trees, the women suddenly disappeared from the camp, scurrying off like beetles and chattering madly.

"Where are they going?" I shouted to Polecat. I had to holler over the roar of the fire and the drumming.

"Back soon, back soon," he assured me. He was worked up to a fine tenseness. In a minute the women reappeared, leading the decorated buffalo ponies.

These were the pride of the tribe, worth many buffalo hides. The horses were sure of foot, catlike as cow ponies for evading the bison at close quarters. And they were, of necessity, swift and long-winded. They were decorated with talismans, painted weirdly, some defying any guess as to their true coloration.

Polecat took his favorite pony, a paint with green stripes and his badger charm painted on each foreleg. He greeted it with a hug of the animal's neck and proceeded to smother it with kisses.

"For you, Rourke," a small voice said. I turned to find Wind on the Waters standing beside me, bareheaded, a tall red pony with her.

"I'm honored," I told her. She looked up as if to say something, her large eyes eager, but she ran off suddenly.

I took the horse by the neck, stroking it in imitation of the others.

"Your medicine bag," Polecat told me, handing me a beaded elkskin bag. This too was an honor. I took it and knotted it into the red pony's mane.

"Your bag must be empty, white boy. What medicine could you have?" It was Yellow Glove and he was painted fiercely; riding his black, he led a wild mustang grotesquely painted, nostrils flaring and dancing on the end of its tether. It was the finest horse I'd ever seen.

"You know I cannot say what medicine I have," I told him. "But we will see how strong it is. This morning."

With a snorting laugh Yellow Glove pulled aside, the mustang following.

"Now," Polecat shouted, and he leaped onto the back of his riding pony, fighting the buffalo pony's lead rope. The buffalo pony, ridden only on a hunt and half wild to begin with, backed toward the fire, stood, and described a half circle. It was a white horse, streaked with faint patches of brown, but painted with vivid green. It appeared a demon rising out of the fire. Polecat roared with appreciation. "He will run them today!"

"Rourke!" Wind in Trees shouted to me. The old man would not ride today, but he beckoned me to him. "That is a fine animal, that red pony. He knows the hunt. Trust to him."

"I will," I promised. I hesitated another moment.

"Rourke!" Polecat was waving to me, the riders were stringing out of the camp, a ghostly procession of painted men and horses in the morning grayness.

"One minute!"

I found what I wanted and got to work quickly. On

the flank of my horse I painted a white circle and on his neck a coiled serpent. Then for luck I pressed my hand into the red dye and left my handprint on his muzzle.

Polecat nodded with approval and together we rode out, following the others through the deep, frost-silvered woods and out onto the plains.

The flatlands shimmered like a thousand mirrors, white upon white and shockingly brilliant. They rolled away toward the flat silver ribbon of the Marias River where redbud trees flared up in bright crimson. The horses were still, even the buffalo ponies, breathing volumes of hot rising steam, their backs and quivering flanks giving off heat as well.

There was no wind and their feathered manes hung limp. Many of them waited, three-legged, as if knowing the rush to battle would come soon. I had never seen them so patient and still before.

The sun sent out runners of gold and purple then shocked our eyes with its first venturing forth, squinting between the twin peaks to the east before triumphantly exploding in white satin brilliance across the snow-smothered earth.

Quail Walker's hand went up.

No one spoke, no one breathed. We could see them afar off, black humps against the winter white. We were upwind and they did not know that death was among them.

I undressed and slid naked onto the back of the red pony, its body warm, trembling with eager anticipation. I threw two half hitches of rawhide around his muzzle—these horses would accept no more rein.

Silently, we walked forward, our ponies sinking into the snow hock-high. There was no sound but a massive bull buffalo grumbling as he lurched to his feet a hundred yards away. A flight of teal winged past rapidly as if fleeing the death stalkers.

I glanced around and saw only apparitions, painted, streaked, and concentrating on only one objective. They were naked warriors in the icy morning, some with five or six arrows in their mouths, a sawed-off flintlock gripped tightly.

They were grisly, sanguine creatures out of prehistory, their eyes fixed hard on the trembling black hulks ahead. Crows and eagles, badgers, bears and lions—signs of magic and of valor coated their ponies and their naked bodies. And I was one of them, my own heart tingling with the animal pleasure of it, the blood urge.

There was a sudden surge forward and then we slapped our heels to the horses. The buffalo, up and running first in one direction then sweeping wide to the south, were forced toward the frozen river. The great ambling beasts ran, blue tongues dangling, rib cages pounding frantically, but we were faster and in a second we were among them.

Polecat fired quickly, and riding his paint pony beside a young cow, he took her at the neck with his musket almost touching her wooly hide. She buckled and went down, bawling.

From the corner of my eye I saw Quail Walker fire just below the hump of a large bull. It turned as if to charge, but its legs went to jelly and it went flat on its face, its massive head thumping hard against the churned earth.

I had a fair shot at a cow with a calf, but wanting a bull, I let her run. The bison were all around us, swarming like great wooly insects. Reaching the river, they turned back, frightened and confused. Yet I did not feel pity for them. We were not running them to frighten them, or to see their blood run, but because the tribe needed meat to last the remaining cold months.

My red horse knew his work and he ran impatiently.

"You want me to do my part!" I laughed. A huge bull bristling with arrows came across our path and the red horse made after him. But this one had been stung by another hunter. I wanted my own.

Soon we were alone, racing across the frozen world, a mammoth bull beside us, his huge head bobbing as he ran. I urged the horse on and he went in closer. I wanted the kill to be clean.

Reaching out with the Henry, I placed the muzzle behind the shoulder, over the heart, and fired. But there were two shots. As the bull stumbled and fell, fatally wounded, the red horse bit angrily at his shoulder and swung his head in a wide arc. The buffalo went down and the horse stumbled but regained its footing.

I slowed the pony gradually and clambered down. Across his shoulder was a deep gouge, a bleeding wound caused by a rifle bullet.

There were three braves riding toward me, whooping joyously. Polecat was among them.

"Is that your bull!" he yelled, swinging down. "A fine one . . ."

"My horse," I interrupted. "Shot."

Polecat looked at the shoulder, frowning. "Sometimes this happens. We are many, close together."

"I was alone," I reminded him. "It was no accident."

Yellow Glove rode up, his horse flecked with blood. He leaped down and laughingly pointed to my bull. "So you do have medicine in your bag!"

"Enough." I stared coldly at him. "Enough to cause a bullet to miss me, perhaps."

Yellow Glove didn't hesitate. He drove a shoulder into me and in a moment had me pinned to the icy earth. He raised a knife and I was helpless.

"Enough!" Polecat held back his arm. "Not today. It is no good. The hunt has gone well; do not ruin it."

"Not today then," Yellow Glove promised. He was sitting on me still, but I felt his muscles go slack. "Not today, but I will finish this."

Then he rose and with one jump was on his pony's back, riding off through the snow, his voice raised in a jubilant resonant shriek.

"Do not provoke him," Polecat advised me. He helped me up. I stood shivering, for the first time feeling the cold. My buffalo lay in a sad brownish heap nearby.

"He tried to kill me," I said.

"You do not know . . ."

"I know. And you know it, too, Polecat."

"Yes," he said. "I know it."

The women had come down onto the plains and they skinned the buffalo as we dressed and ate, for our hunters' portion, the hot raw liver of our buffalo.

"You have no squaw," Polecat told me. "You will have to skin your own."

"No. I will do it." It was Wind on the Waters and she looked defiantly at Yellow Glove, who was perched sideways on his pony's back, blood staining his still bare chest.

"You will not! Girl, you will be my wife in the spring. You are forbidden!"

"Wind on the Waters," I said, touching her slight shoulder. "Please don't. Not if it will cause trouble."

"You are afraid of him?"

"No." I said it and I meant it. I had a respect for his strength and the knowledge that he would probably kill me quickly in a hand-to-hand fight, but I was not afraid of Yellow Glove. "I'm not afraid of him."

"And I am not either," she said with a toss of her head. "And no man but my father can yet forbid me. I will skin your buffalo."

I watched her walk off, her buckskin dress dusting the snow. She went to my kill, knelt, and started to work. She worked hard, efficiently, and with a will. I admired the girl. More, I was beginning to feel an affection for her. What she had done was a giving thing, and it warmed my heart. I thought on that for a minute, enjoying the thought. Until I turned and saw the cold, killing eyes of Yellow Glove fixed unwaveringly on me.

"In the spring," Polecat told me in a low voice, "you will have to go."

"In the spring," I said, loud enough for Yellow Glove to hear, "I will leave the lodge of my friends, the Piegan. But not before. I won't let my enemies drive me from the camp of my friends."

SEVEN

Wind in Trees was alone in his lodge as I entered. The old man appeared frail, his eyes unnaturally bright, his hands overly large on his thin arms. His face was framed with coarse white hair. He caught the look of surprise on my face.

"I grow old fast, Rourke." He waved a hand in a gesture of futility. "Too much sick, too many long winters."

"It will soon grow warmer."

"Perhaps not for me. Sit down. Sit down, Rourke, let us talk. I have grown fond of you. And so has Wind on the Waters."

"And I have grown fond of you."

He invited me to sit down and I took a place on the brown bearskin robe near the dwindling fire.

"Now I want to talk of my daughter," Wind in Trees said. He paused, stroking his white, long-stemmed clay pipe. Finally, taking small puffs of blue tobacco smoke, he began.

"You have made trouble with Yellow Glove, Rourke. Perhaps," he said, his eyes narrowing, "I misunderstood. I thought you knew the Piegan ways."

"I know your ways."

"Wind on the Waters must marry Yellow Glove. It is not good for a man to be alone. Who will cook his food and sweep his lodge? Who will skin his buffalo and make his moccasins?

"And what of a young girl with neither father nor husband to watch over her? Who will hunt for her? Who will hunt for Wind on the Waters? Will you, Rourke!"

I didn't answer, not knowing what to say. The old man studied me closely, his piercing gaze searching out my eyes which refused to meet his. Finally, he shrugged. "You must not interfere."

"But she is young. So young!" I protested.

"No! Not for Piegan brides. Thirteen years she has walked among her people. For those years I watched over the girl. Sheltered her. Defended her. Now . . . I feel death's finger beckoning to me in the cold nights, Rourke. She will need a husband. After the Sun Dance, when the blossoms are on the trees, she will marry."

"She doesn't want him," I explained adamantly. "Wind on the Waters does not find Yellow Glove . . . suitable."

"Suitable! She doesn't find him suitable? He is strong, Yellow Glove. And a good hunter. A warrior. Would you have her live with a weakling who could not provide? Or would you have her be like certain whites who marry as their passions dictate? They forget that life is long and hard with many other purposes than passion.

"No," he said firmly, "he is suitable." The old man closed his eyes heavily, shaking his head wearily. "But so are you, Rourke."

"Me!" I laughed, without meaning to laugh.

"Yes. There are ways. As you have noticed, the girl favors you. And you also are a fine hunter and a warrior. That has been proven to me. But," he said cautiously, "you would have to fight Yellow Glove to the death."

"No," I told him, "I cannot do that."

"You are afraid?"

"No, Wind in Trees. She is just a girl."

"And you little more than a boy, Clay Rourke."

"The whites . . ."

"Forget the whites! Stay with us, Rourke," he said, and he meant it, his dark eyes nearly pleading. "Forget this hunt for your father's killer. Here, among the Piegan, Wind on the Waters is not too young. And here you are already a man. She will grow to be a beautiful woman, Rourke. And a devoted wife."

"I think so as well. But I can't do what you suggest. My father's killer must be found. Would you have me forget this debt? I cannot go against my upbringing."

"You are white," he said with a heavy sigh, placing his pipe down in the cup made for it.

"Yes, I am white."

"Then go, Rourke," he said softly, his eyes downcast. "Now. Before the Sun Dance, before Yellow Glove has killed you."

"Wind in Trees." I stood and fumbled for the words. "I cannot . . ."

"Go Rourke! Do not come again. Go to the white world and leave us to ours."

I turned and walked from the lodge without looking back. He was right. It was time. I had no business meddling in their affairs unless I was willing myself to make the same commitment Yellow Glove was willing to make. The snows were few now; although the high passes were clogged with snow, travel was possible, and I had known it for some time.

She was standing there as I drew back the reddish blanket on the door of the lodge.

Just for a moment Wind on the Waters's eyes stayed on mine—wide, glossed with tears, shocked. Then she turned and ran into the pinewoods. She had been listening.

I started to call out but choked off the cry. What was there to say? She was young, too young to understand. Perhaps she had spoken to her father. She had wanted me for her husband, and it was flattering, touching—but impossible.

"I have your pack made up," Polecat told me. He smiled weakly and slapped my shoulder, letting his hand linger there for a moment.

"You knew?"

"Yes," he said, "and I could guess your reply. It is for the best, Rourke. What will you do now?" he asked after a pause.

I had been thinking for some time on just that. I had had all of the long winter to ponder it, to turn over every possibility.

"I had planned on going to Colorado," I told him. "But now I have another thought. In Oregon I have family—my mother's people live there. I never knew them . . . not well enough to know them on the street, but Pa used to talk of them."

"You will stay with them?"

"I don't know. There was some sort of trouble between my mother's family and Pa. There are three brothers, I understand. Two of them are merchants, and the other, Nate Thatcher, is a sailing ship's master."

"A ship's master! A captain!"

"That's right." I had told Polecat the entire story, that there was a captain involved in the plot to kill my father, and he had seen immediately what I was getting at.

At first I had been positive that the trouble had its origins in Colorado, since my father was bound for there. But he had known not a soul in that territory, at least he had never spoken of anyone before. Not until this business deal—if that was what it actually was—with the man named Hewitt.

But he had spoken bitterly of the Thatcher brothers. I knew he had fought Jay Thatcher with fists, nearly killing him just months before we had left for Montana. I hadn't been so young that I wasn't impressed by the sight of my father, slumped over the kitchen table, hands swollen and cut, cursing the man.

"He slandered your mother, Clayborne," he told me through raw lips. "And I won't take that. Most anything else, but not that."

Polecat nodded as I finished. "So, we must ride west to Oregon."

"You mean to ride with me?"

"Yes. If you will have me. I wish to see beyond the mountains, this great sea I have heard about."

"Of course you're welcome." I put my hands on his sturdy shoulders. "I'll be happy to have your company."

"Your horse is ready, Rourke. . . . If you will give me a minute to say good-bye to my brother."

"Of course. My horse?" I was puzzled.

"The red horse. The buffalo horse. Wind in Trees sent it for you this morning."

"Then he already had guessed the outcome of our meeting."

"So it seems." Polecat's broad face was thoughtful. "Wind in Trees has lived long; he knows it is not easy for a man to change his beliefs."

"I must thank him for the horse."

"No, Rourke. Leave it as it is. He would have no answer for your thanks. Let us go. Let us go to your Oregon, or wherever you wish, but let us go." Polecat's normally affable face was drawn. His heavy lips were tightly compressed. I nodded.

"All right."

I waited as Polecat said his good-byes. As I did, arranging my pack and checking the red horse's hoofs, I glanced toward the shadows, everywhere, hoping for one last look at Wind on the Waters, one last chance to speak and tell her that I had not refused her because I did not care for her, but because it was not the way of my people. But I never saw her.

"We go." Polecat slipped fluidly onto the back of his dapple-gray pony and without waiting for me to speak, he jerked the horse's head around, toward the west and the towering blue mountains.

We rode easily through the still, cold morning. The sunlight danced in the treetops and sparkled in the dew of the grass, making thousands of brilliant jewels. The red horse was eager, moving forward quickly as if anticipating the challenge of the high blue mountains, relishing it.

Polecat rode just at my flank, and I thought he rode a little uneasily. Maybe he was beginning to have second thoughts about leaving his people. From time to time I caught him turning his head back toward the Piegan village now hidden in the blue spruce deep in the river-cut valley.

We camped at noon beside a foaming waterfall rushing out of the sheer, water-glazed white rock. Polecat had gone into the woods for five minutes and returned with a fat porcupine.

"No trouble," Polecat said. "Good food for man

with no weapons. This one I catch quick, hit him with a stick."

He roasted the porky, daintily working around the quills as he skinned it. The liver was surprisingly large, amazingly good. We drank from the stream and rested an hour before moving on.

The shadows grew long early in the afternoon as the sun faded behind the timbered reaches of the mountains. Polecat had stopped beside a fork in the little-used trail.

"What is it?"

"Look, you see." He pointed at the damp, dark earth and I saw it too.

"White men. Three horses."

"Two men, I think. This one is a pack animal," Polecat guessed. "They go where we wish to go."

"Trappers?"

"No, I do not think so." Polecat shook his head definitely.

There was nothing particularly alarming about finding the tracks. But this was high up, desolate country where the winds tore the trees from their desperate moorings and the snows clotted the passes. It was a little-used, little-known trail we rode and there was little travel anywhere along this part of the country. Polecat did not like the feel of it, and my instincts were with him.

"We will take the other trail," Polecat announced suddenly. "I think we do best to avoid these men."

"Is it a good trail?"

"Bad. Very bad, Rourke. But I do not like this sign."

We rode then to the north, winding along the faint scar of a path leading into the deep gorges and along the gray, timberless slopes where wind-battered crags

jutted out into space, the ice deep in the raw cre-
vasses, the snow heavy on the ground. We paused
again on a high, desolate knoll. Polecat looked back
the way we had come, along that bleak high pass.

"You think the men will come?" I asked. I was
puzzled by Polecat's apprehensions. Whoever the two
white men had been, they would have no way of
knowing we had come behind them. Surely they
wouldn't have doubled back onto this trail. We had
nothing to steal worth the taking but the horses.

"The white men?" Polecat asked, turning back to
me. "I do not know. But Yellow Glove will come. He
will come."

"But why?" The idea hadn't occurred to me. "I
have gone from the camp of the Piegan. He will have
the girl. All is as it was before."

"No," Polecat answered. "It is not as it was before.
He has not forgotten. He spoke of it—of wanting to
kill you, and once he has spoken he must do it."

"Then we had better ride."

"Yes."

Polecat took the lead then, his gray feeling its way
down a treacherous, rock-strewn portion of the feeble
trail. The wind blew as if to cut us in half. Far away
the brilliant sun nestled into its gray, sodden bed,
glowing a harsh red.

"Is that why you came?" I asked him. The trail had
grown dim and we rode on only to search for a place
secure enough for our camp.

"What is that, Rourke?"

"Is that why you chose to ride with me, Polecat?
Because of Yellow Glove? Because you knew I would
never find this trail?"

"I rode because you are my friend, Rourke." I

could not see his face in the darkness. "We dare not ride any longer."

"All right." I could see that he wanted no more talk of his reasons for coming, but to me it was all too clear, and I was grateful. We huddled in a tiny hollow, partially sheltered by some scrub, weather-broken ponderosa pine. Our horses stood close together, tails to the shriek of the wind, and we sat close to our tiny, wind-buffeted fire.

The fire burned low and we let it, despite our hunger for warmth. The wind chanted in the pines and now and then a branch or a whole tree came down, crashing to the frozen earth, sending chills up my spine. I had my buffalo robe over my head, with my Henry inside the tent to prevent the action from freezing as the temperature plummeted.

It was dark as the fire withered and extinguished itself. Dark so that I could not see Polecat or even the huge granite outcropping overhead. Nothing.

I heard a small noise.

Not a familiar sound, like rock breaking loose from a shattered outcropping or the boughs of the pine whipping free or the changeless roar of the wind guns.

I held perfectly still. Polecat, if he was still there, said nothing, and I held my tongue as well. My thumb was on the hammer of my rifle and my muscles bunched, growing tauter with each passing moment. Nothing.

Then I heard it again, and I scooted back farther into the dismembered trunks of the frozen forest. The clouds sheeted over the sky. If there was a moon we saw none of it. I felt, rather than heard, someone or something beside me and I rolled over, bringing my rifle barrel up.

"No, Rourke."

It was Polecat. Somehow he had slipped out of the camp and crawled up the draw behind. He tapped my arm and pointed back toward our camp. Something sparked, went out, sparked again, and took hold. In seconds a small fire was burning.

"Come, we go," Polecat whispered, bending close to my ear. I nodded and crawled after him, inching toward the camp, the icy wind stiffening my fingers and joints, biting at my face. We were within ten feet of the clearing when I saw clearly who had started the fire.

"Wind on the Waters!"

"Yes?"

She turned around innocently, her eyes open, her lips parted in a welcoming smile. A weary paint pony stood picketed near ours, and on its back was a large pack.

"You must leave," I told her.

"No. I must go with you."

"It's crazy. I don't want you! Tell her, Polecat!"

The Indian shrugged and, I thought, grinned a little. I could have killed him for it.

"You will want me, Rourke. When I am older, if not now." Wind on the Waters busied herself cooking some sort of broth made with dried salmon.

"Now Yellow Glove will certainly come," I said gloomily.

"Why so sad?" Wind on the Waters asked. "You will kill him. Then we will be free of him."

"I don't want to kill him! You're the one I wish to be free of. I thought that was clear."

"You will change your mind. Here, have some soup. It will warm you."

"I don't want it."

"First you turn your back on a fine girl," Polecat said lightly, "now on a fish chowder. You are a strange man, Rourke. But, perhaps I will understand you someday. For now, I will eat some soup if you do not mind."

I took my robe and rifle and went away from the fire. Cold as I was I left my head uncovered; tired as I was I did not sleep. I watched the two Piegan at the fire and even considered for one foolish moment abandoning them, and trying it on my own. I doubted I could lose them if I tried, however. And I did not know the way.

It bothered me that Polecat seemed so unconcerned about it all. It was enough to make me suspect that he knew what the girl would do all along. And I . . . I knew what Yellow Glove would do for a certainty.

Somehow I fell off to sleep, my head drooping, my rifle still clenched firmly in my hand. Despite the clamor of the wind and the wooden dueling of the tree limbs, the cold and the uncertainty, I fell off to sleep. And when I awakened they were in the camp, their weapons on me.

EIGHT

———•———

I wedged my eyes open. There were two dark silhouetted figures in front of me as I struggled to my feet. One of them shot out a hand which took me by the throat as my rifle was torn from my grasp. There was no one else in camp. Wind on the Waters and Polecat had gone!

"Who are you?" I panted.

I looked from one face to the other. White faces, they were, but ones I had never seen. One of them, nearly toothless and in dirty buckskins, grinned back.

"Friends of yourn, boy. Friends."

"I don't know you."

"All men are friends," the man in buckskins said idiotically.

"Fine," I said. "Give me my gun, friend."

Sabers of brilliant sunlight cut through the crystal morning, backlighting the deep green of the scattered pines, glossing the ice on the rocks with a cold sheen.

"We aren't that good of friends, young man," the other stranger said. This one was tall, narrow hipped, with a nervous mouth. He was dressed as a cowhand, but his boots were finely made. He sucked at a half-cold cigarette and nodded.

"What's your name?" I asked.

"You are a suspicious boy," the tall man said slowly.

He watched me with appraising, intelligent dark eyes.

"Don't tell him," the buckskinned man said. This one appeared to be not only stupid, but downright harebrained. He squatted, sucked at a straw, stood, rocked on his heels, and shifted his hat three different times in the space of a few minutes.

"Yule Haslitt DeLong." The tall man said it slowly, with a touch of pride. "And I mean you no harm, boy. This here with me is Bake Jepitt. Friend of mine, and one with sand."

The oaf glowed with pride as his friend described him in that way. I nodded curtly to both of them.

"Rourke. Clay Rourke."

"I knew it." DeLong nodded and examined me more closely. "I knew it," he repeated. "No doubt from your features. Where in hell is your daddy, boy? I'm up from Leadville. He was supposed to be in last September, but he never showed."

"He's dead. Ambushed. You say you're from Leadville. Know a man called Hewitt, do you?"

DeLong hesitated, scratching his chin. "Yes," he drawled. "I guess I do know him. That's my given name. I had me some trouble in other parts. So I switched my name around a little. I'm Hewitt, and I was a friend of your daddy's. Knowed him in the War between the States. And together we planned on making some money in cattle."

"My father didn't have any money to speak of," I said dubiously.

"No. But I had me some from a timber tract that went right for me last year. I knew Rourke—your pa—had some land up north here. I figured with some cattle, with his graze, we could fatten them cows up fine and tap a market that's been ignored."

DeLong, or Hewitt as my daddy had known him, handed me back my rifle. "Thanks," I said. "I feel a might more secure with that. Tell me, DeLong, did you ever hear tell of a man called the Captain?"

"The Captain?" DeLong thought a minute, then shrugged, glancing at Bake Jepitt. "No, not in my recollection. Why?"

"I believe he's the one had my daddy killed."

"Don't recall the name and I knew most the folks your pa knew, except them up to Oregon, of course." He nudged Jepitt who had fallen to staring at his rifle barrel. "You know of a man called the Captain? Bake?"

"Huh? No. Never heard of him." Bake's mind seemed to wander frequently. I caught him now squatting down, tracing figures in the dirt.

"That where you're heading, boy? Oregon?" De-Long asked abruptly.

"Yes." My eyes were on Jepitt.

"Maybe we'll ride on aways. Be all right?"

"I reckon. If you're of a mind."

"There was two others here," Bake said, suddenly rising to his feet. "Told you there was three riding together."

DeLong regarded me curiously. His eyes flickered to the underbrush and the surrounding rocks. "Where are they?" He asked in a demanding tone. I shrugged.

"I don't know. Guess they heard you riding in."

"Indians, ain't they?"

"Bow-Piegan. Friends of mine."

"Hell, boy," DeLong laughed. "I don't mean you no harm. You can call them in."

"I guess they'll come in when they want to. I'm not sure where they are, anyway." That was the truth.

But I did have me an idea Polecat wasn't far off. I believed I had caught a shadow moving off to my left, behind DeLong, among the broken trees.

"Make some coffee, Bake," DeLong said. The man grunted a reply and went off to do it. I sat pondering as the wind began to pick up again, rattling in the trees.

This man said he had business with my pa. Said it, but it proved nothing. On the other hand, it might just as well have been true. DeLong, as I caught his face now, seemed a hard man, a man who had seen some worry and who had been over the mountain and down the trail. But that meant nothing except to say that he was like most of the men west of the big river at that time. My own father would probably have appeared much the same, perhaps a little more frank, more given to smile. All the same, I meant to keep my eyes open and my rifle to hand.

"You want some?" Bake Jeppit asked. He was holding a pot with a towel. I nodded. I wasn't used to drinking coffee, having been with the Piegan, and I hadn't much liked it as a boy, but the smell was tempting. He poured it black and strong.

"We'd best get to lower ground with this weather coming in," DeLong suggested. "We'll see you over the mountains, Clay. I owed your daddy. Owed him quite a bit."

The wind shifted a little and I heard something I did not like. With the coffee still in my hand I glanced back over my shoulder. Yellow Glove!

He dove from the brush and his knife glinted in the sunlight, already swinging in a cutting arc; he hurled himself at me.

I threw myself down, rolled, thrust up with the

muzzle of the Henry. There was a shot and Yellow Glove folded up. He got to his knees.

"My woman." He grunted, clutching his stomach. His hand came away bloody. His abdomen was leaking red. But he came on, staggering to his feet as he came nearer, his face a tangle of hate and anger, pain and determination. I'll never know if I could have shot him. DeLong's handgun barked again and Yellow Glove pitched forward drunkenly, his legs twitching. He managed to lift his head again, but he was dead by then.

"That your friend?" DeLong asked.

"No, but I knew him. He was in my tribe."

"You sound sorry about it," DeLong said. He poked three fresh cartridges into his Colt.

"I am."

"Hell," Bake Jepitt snorted, "you a fool, boy. That Injun was meaning to lay you open."

I stood watching Yellow Glove's body. I never thought it would happen like that. I thought we would go at it hand to hand. I guess, probably, he would have come out on top. But I didn't like it that way.

"I am coming!" A voice came from out of the pinewoods. Bake Jepitt pulled his rifle free of the scabbard. I put my hand on his arm.

"Don't."

"This your friend?"

"No. But he won't fight."

I waited. Then Quail Walker came slowly forward, his pony's head bowed, Yellow Glove's horse trailing behind him. He was naked to the waist despite the cold, the wind beating down his feathered topknot.

"I will take him."

"Do it, Quail Walker. He was an honorable enemy."

"Kid," Bake Jepitt snarled. "Better do this one too. He'll be back."

"No, he won't."

Quail Walker was bending over his friend. He picked him up awkwardly, the blood staining him, and pushed him up over the pony's back. Then, without another word, he turned and rode slowly off over the bleak landscape, white trees on white rock, moving ahead of the coming gray clouds toward the village of the Piegan.

"You're a strange boy," Bake said, shaking his head dumbly.

"He don't mean nothing," DeLong apologized. "It's just that Bake and me . . . I guess we seen too many soft-hearted people pay for it."

"Doc French," Bake said.

"What?"

"Doc French. Man we knowed. Patched up a man he'd had at in a gunfight. Took him home, kept him, and fed him. Soon as he was on his feet, he back shot the Doc."

"This was different."

"No different. Man says you're his enemy, take him at his word," DeLong told me. "That's the way the Indian sees it. That's the way I see it. Could be you layin' over that pony's back."

"That's not the way my pa saw things," I said, and I said it hotly. "Nor is it the way he taught me to see things."

"Yeah. And look where it got him," Bake said.

"Leave the kid alone," DeLong said softly. He holstered his pistol and took off his hat, shaking his head to clear his eyes of his long, dark hair before setting it back on. He drank his cup of coffee in two short gulps.

"What'd he mean about his woman?" Bake Jepitt asked. His beady little eyes were bright. He chewed on a dry biscuit as he sucked at his coffee. He wiped his mouth with a dirty, buckskinned sleeve. "He said somethin' about his woman."

"Nothing," I replied.

"A woman out here, Yule," Bake said. He snorted again and sucked at his drink. "A squaw woman."

"Knock it off."

"She around here?" Bake leered at me and set to looking around the camp perimeter. I had never seen a man look more the animal than he did at that moment, his jaw slack, his eyes glazed and tiny.

"Yes," a voice said. "But I am not Yellow Glove's woman. I am Rourke's." Slowly, Wind on the Waters came forward, her hands clasped before her, her small steps noiseless on the hard earth.

"Who are you?" DeLong wanted to know.

"Wind on the Waters," she said, and she said it proudly, her chin held high. DeLong laughed out loud, and Bake let out a disappointed groan.

"Hell, it's only a kid." He looked quizzically at me. "That the way you favor 'em, Rourke?"

I flushed and turned toward him.

"Indians take 'em young," DeLong said quickly. "Come have some coffee, girl."

Hesitantly, Wind on the Waters did as she was told. It was awhile before Polecat came in, his musket loose in his hand, but obviously ready to be snapped up for a quick shot if need be.

"And a one-eyed Injun!" Bake laughed.

I was developing a definite dislike for this man, but there was no sense in causing trouble now. Bake Jepitt, from what I had seen and he had said, was a man not averse to killing.

"My friend, Polecat."

"DeLong." Yule DeLong stuck out a hand and Polecat took it as a matter of form, it seemed. His musket did not leave his hand. After nodding at Bake Jepitt, he retreated a little ways to a smooth, low rock and sat there, watching and listening.

We crested out the mountain that day, and for the next week we rode slowly to the south and west, with each day dawning brighter, warmer in the high country, the road broadening to a comfortable high meadow passage, and ahead of us we could see, in the clarity of the blue distance, the Bitter Root range where Montana ended and the Divide began its slope down to the sea.

"We'll see you through to Bitter Root," Yule De-Long said.

"Grateful for the company," I said. Though I hadn't got over my distaste for Bake Jepitt, I had come to respect the tall, self-confident Yule DeLong. He seemed to know almost as much of wilderness living as the Piegan.

"You needn't ever worry about scurvy long as you're in spruce country. The young needles are a bit starchy, but they keep the scurvy off. Learned that from the Arapaho."

When I looked at him oddly, he replied, "You're not the only man ever stayed among the Indians, you know. Hell, I'll bet I know half a hundred myself who've stayed among the various people, some marrying and staying. A white man alone has most always been welcome; it's when they come in numbers that the Indian gets his back up, and can't blame 'em much for that."

We usually ate early in the mornings, in the chill gray of that time before sun up, skipped a nooning unless we found good grass or water for the horses, and tucked it in at sundown. The days were short, but full of excitement. We counted elk by the hundreds, their magnificent racks still in velvet, fished when we wished, using string and a bone snag, and swept across the sweet meadows where the flowers spread out in yellow, golden carpets.

"I think we get some berries?" Wind on the Waters suggested.

"Sounds good. Yule?"

"Go ahead, it's a weary day."

We had stopped at the base of a naked outcropping on the edge of a broad expanse of meadows where golden marmot played, deer watered at a low, crystal pond, and ducks, returning to the north country, winged over.

"You do not fight me so now, Rourke," the girl said.

"No. What can I do? Tie you up and leave you? You are going to come, no matter what, I see that now. But why, I don't know."

"Because you will want me, Rourke. I know this." She touched her breast with her fingertips and smiled winningly. "You will want me. So I follow."

We had climbed the bare knoll to a place where a tangle of serviceberry and elderberry wound together with wild plum and dense, brilliant fern. Together we sat, breathing the cold air, taking in all of it—the long stretches of grassland cupped in the foothills, and beyond the jagged ice-capped mountains.

"Are you ever afraid, Clay Rourke?"

"Afraid?" I thought a minute. "Most times, maybe. But I don't worry on it."

"I am afraid," she said, "for you. You hunt to kill. And it will get you killed."

"Before I have decided to marry you?" I asked with a smile, but she shook her head worriedly.

"I do not want you dead. This DeLong . . ."

"DeLong's all right."

"You do not know him. I see the way he watches you."

"That's just his way, Wind on the Waters."

"Why does he help us?" she demanded.

"He was a friend of my father's. That's the only reason. If he meant me harm, he would have killed me long ago."

"Not while Polecat is alive," she insisted. Suddenly, after a pensive moment she snatched up her tote sack and went to her gathering. DeLong had found some chicory while we were on the knoll and he showed me what it looked like, pretty it was with those delicate blue flowers.

"Relative of the dandelion," DeLong told me.

Bake cocked his head. It set me to wondering too—how would a man know something like that unless he had been educated in botany?

There were things about DeLong I couldn't fit together. A savage man, at times he was unusually gentle. Once we all stopped for an hour while he splinted the leg of a mallard we came across, flopping on the grass.

"This creature—what harm will it ever do us?" He said it mournfully as he wound the leg with thread.

Bake Jepitt looked away with disgust, but I noticed Polecat watching with amazement.

Time to time DeLong would come out with words

or mentions that surprised me. Most of the time he talked like a cowhand or a lumberjack, both of which he had been, but again he'd tell me which stars were which, pointing out Sirius and that big red star, Betelgeuse; and he'd tell me which were planets and how many moons they had and such.

"I love it, boy," he said one night as we made dry camp, all sitting in the dark stillness. "A man can learn nature from the inside out or from the outside in. He can know it like the Indians do: the herbs, the way to fashion your clothing, to heal a wound, and to find food where there's none. Or, he can learn about it through books. . . . I wanted to know it all at one time. Then, when I found out that was impossible, I learned as much as I could and sat back to be amazed by her."

At each stop, each watering hole or night camp, DeLong also held another kind of class. The first time it startled me. I looked up from drinking to see him over me with a gun drawn.

"You know what this is?" he asked, turning the Colt over.

"Yes."

"Do you know what makes it tick? How to take it apart and put it back together? Could you make a spring out of raw material for her?"

"No, I reckon not," I said with a faint smile. There was an out and out odd look on his dark, sharp face. His eyes were on mine, but beyond them.

"Can you make her dance while she sings, boy?"

"Sir?"

"Like this." He holstered his pistol, turned a quarter away and his hand flashed, the pistol coming up and firing in one easy, startling fast jump. The pop of the discharge curled my hair. Yule dropped the gun into his holster. "Dance while she sings," he repeated.

"I never had me a handgun. Not one that was actually mine," I told him. "Not much use for pot shooting."

Without another word he took off his holster and handed it to me, the gun still in it. "Take this. Your pa gave me his once," he added. "At a time when I needed one or I would've died."

"When was that?"

"Take it," DeLong said. Then he turned and walked away. I stood holding the gunbelt dumbly in the failing light. I saw Bake Jepitt standing in the trees, a look of exasperation on his face. He walked over, took Yule by the arm and said something. Yule shook him off.

"His pa saved my bacon," I heard him say.

From then on I wore that gun, and from then on I learned to handle it, the movements coming slowly at first, my thumb not going smoothly to the hammer, my aim too studied. But it came, and when it began to come right, I could feel that pistol fairly leap into my hand and fire of its own volition at whatever target I had in mind.

I was getting cocky with it, I guess. Once I drew and took a flying woodcock with it from the saddle. Yule DeLong rode quickly beside me, his long hair flying, and he took my bridle.

"Learn your limits, Clay. And learn there's others who can go beyond them."

He looked hard into my eyes and then without glancing backward he drew his pistol and thumbed through five shots at my woodcock, hitting it each time, tearing the bird to chunks of meat. Angrily, he reloaded and put his pistol away.

"Soon rid of him. Better off," Polecat said in a low voice.

"Better off," I agreed. I liked Yule, but feared his moods, his seething energy hidden just under the skin of amiability. I didn't draw my own handgun again until we parted company.

It was two days later at the Wingshaw Pass where the Bitter Roots broke open, tumbling over down toward Idaho. Suddenly Yule DeLong pulled up. He stepped down and went to his pack.

"What's up?"

"We're pulling out," he said.

"Like that?"

"Like that. It's come time. I said we'd see you to the Bitter Roots."

"Thanks," I said. "Thanks, Yule."

"It's nothing. You go on ahead to Oregon. Find what you're looking for there. Keep your eyes open and learn. He paused, looking around hesitantly.

"You're a young man, Clay. Take some time to learn. Get some schooling. Don't start riding that vengeance trail. It'll get you a lot of sleepless nights and in the end a belly full of lead. I know, believe me."

"I got to do it."

"Well—think on it. You get some learning. You're a bright fellow, make use of it. Here."

He stretched out his hand and shoved ten double eagles into my pack. "Owed it to your pa," he muttered. Then he stepped quickly back into his saddle and rode off with Bake Jepitt turning back to watch me over his shoulder, saying something angrily about the gold.

"Well." I scratched my head. "Two hundred dollars. I told you he was a good man under it all."

"Better off rid of him, Rourke," Polecat said. "Better off. That man—he will kill."

NINE

———◆———

We came on to Port Keyes the first day of May. Awed, we sat together on the grassy hillocks above the town and studied the majestic, sweeping ocean. The smell of salt was in the air, the rich and timeless odor of sea plants and kelp drying on the shores. Gulls wheeled overhead, white, calling raucously. Terns and sandpipers raced on stilt legs over the low dunes as Polecat, Wind on the Waters, and I rode into Port Keyes from the south.

There wasn't much of the town. A church with a squat steeple, painted fresh white, a number of weather-beaten buildings along the dark wharves, and back toward the residential section a row of neat houses, all white but for one—a yellow, two-story house with gingerbread on it stuck by itself on a hill. Fenced around in wrought iron, it struck a sudden chord of remembrance.

"That's the house," I told Polecat.

"Big house. Very big. Your uncle is a rich man," Polecat ventured.

We rode slowly through the streets. The day had gone to haze, cooling fast. Along the streets men in pea jackets smoked pipes, some drinking ale in front of a tavern. They were whiskered seamen, brawny men of the sea unlike any I had seen. Here and there was a cowhand, a jack, a merchant, but they looked some out of place. We were more out of place than any of them. Straggling up the main street, we drew curious stares. A rawboned kid toting a worn Henry rifle and a one-eyed Indian dressed in a manner unique to these Oregon eyes . . . and a small, proud Indian girl.

In a few minutes we had attracted half the kids in town. They ran behind us screaming and pointing. A couple of them threw rocks. I saw a big, surly-eyed kid with red hair leaning casually against a post. He was about my age and he spat as we passed, pushing his cap forward.

"That the Thatcher place?"

"Who wants to know?"

"I do." I said it quietly, and he was about to give me a smart remark when his eyes caught the Henry in my off hand and the Colt I wore on my hip.

"That's it," he growled. Miles Thatcher's place, anyway. Nate, he ain't to town and Jay, well, he is but he ain't entertaining."

Nate was the one I wanted to see. The ship's master.

Jay, from what I knew, was a brawler and a drinker. Probably the kid had meant he was off on a binge. I would have to make do with Miles Thatcher, who was a merchant of some sort. We drew up at the iron gate.

"What will you do?" Polecat asked.

"I don't know." Suddenly, it all seemed a crazy impulse. I didn't belong here, hunting my uncle. I belonged in the faraway mountains with the Piegan and the free wind. But I was here.

I took a deep breath and swung the gate open,

Polecat and Wind on the Waters following me through.

"Yes." The door squeaked open reluctantly, and a tight, pinched face peered through the crack. The house smelled of velvet and of furniture oil.

"I'm looking for Nate Thatcher."

"He isn't here," the woman said. From somewhere long ago and far away her face struck me with its familiar angles. Maybe it was only the old tintypes of the Thatcher family I recalled, but I thought I remembered this woman's sour expression, those pursed, lined lips.

"Where is he . . . if I may inquire?"

"Who are you?" The door had not opened another inch.

"I'm . . ."

"Never mind! Oh, Lord, don't think it doesn't show! I can see you clearly now. A Rourke. Son of Jeb Rourke."

"And of your daughter, Mrs. Thatcher," I reminded her.

"Disgrace that was! Disgrace. Go on out of here, boy. Leave before Nate or one of his brothers catches you here." Suddenly her eyes caught Wind on the Waters and Polecat standing waiting with the horses. "That where you've been? With the red Indians? Go back with them then, boy. Go on out of here."

The door slammed shut and the big house was utterly silent. A cold, damp wind was blowing off the ocean, the wisps of fog running close to the ground, curling into the forest.

I closed and latched the iron gate behind me. We rode at a walk away from the big yellow house.

"Now we go?" Polecat asked.

"No. Now we start the hunt."

"I am cold."

Wind on the Waters's voice was tiny, quavering.

We were nearing the outskirts of town again, the light failing fast.

"It's not that cold," I said cautiously. It worried me. An Indian is bred in a community setting where death is accepted, where there is no room for grumblers or slackers, and little time to listen to complainers. We had just come over some of the coldest high country on earth, the snow still deep in some of the canyons, the wind like to tear us in half, and not once had she complained.

"She's sick!"

I had caught her face in the yellow light from a saloon window. She was pale as death, hanging desperately to her pony's mane.

I reached out to steady her, but as I did she toppled from her horse's back, falling to the street. Polecat and I were to her in a second.

"Very hot," Polecat said, touching her forehead. He glanced up at me anxiously.

"We'll get her inside . . . somewhere." I picked her up, her weight infinitesimal in my arms. I turned hurriedly, looking up and down the street. "In here!"

"They will not . . ."

"They'll have a room!" I snapped.

I kicked open the door to the saloon and carried her into the hot, close room. Men glanced up from their cards, drinks half hoisted to their mustached lips. The bartender made a move toward me, but I stopped him.

"I got a sick girl here, and I need a room to put her in."

"Put her in a teepee!" a hoarse voice jeered.

"Boy, we can't have no Indians in here."

"She's a sick girl. Show me a bed to put her in. And somebody get a doctor, if you've got one."

No one moved. I looked across their faces—curious, some of them, others were concerned, some only amused. But none of them moved.

"Bartender!"

"It's illegal to have an Indian in here," he said in exasperation. I nodded grimly. Without moving Wind on the Waters I snaked out my Colt, and it looked as big as anyone else's.

"I guess shootin's illegal, too, but there's gonna be some shootin' if you don't find me a place for this girl."

"I don't take well to bein' bulled, boy," the bartender said. A thick-shouldered man with a broken nose, he had the look of an old curly wolf on him. We stood there looking at each other, my thumb down hard on the hammer of my pistol. He had his thick hands on the bar, his sleeves rolled up over his massive forearms. There was no backdown in him. I'd seen men like him before. They'd sooner be shot than take a step backward. The tension was thick. The room was so quiet we all twitched when a sallow-faced cardplayer cleared his throat.

"I'll take care of her, Earl," a voice said, and I turned to see a woman of around forty, her hair stained with henna till it was an unnatural red, her face powdered white. But her hands and eyes were gentle. Wiping the cold sweat from her face with her lace kerchief, she looked closely at Wind on the Waters.

"You don't have to, Liv," the bartender said.

"I know I don't have to, Earl!" Her voice crackled, but softened immediately. "Come on, boy, bring her along."

I followed her into a narrow hallway, the bar behind us returning to its noisy pandemonium.

"In here." The woman, Liv, swung open the door to a small, neat room. She turned on a lamp, blowing out the match thoughtfully. Her eyes were soft blue, but businesslike. Her face showed the lines of too many late nights, too many drinks.

"I'll get this dress off. It's my best," she said, wiping her hand over the green satin dress she wore. I nodded and she disappeared into a tiny adjoining room, returning in a plain cotton dress, her hair knotted back severely.

"Get on down to the doctor's," she ordered me. "He's over the dry goods store. There's a shingle, you won't miss him."

Before I had gotten out of the room, she had filled a basin from an inside pump and placed a damp cloth on Wind on the Waters's forehead and begun pulling off her clothing. "Get!"

Out in the hall Polecat waited, squatting next to the door. The bartender Earl was there, too, wiping his hands on his apron as he came down the hall, moving like a bear.

"I don't have time for trouble now, Earl."

"And I don't either, kid," he growled. "If it's all right with Liv, it's all right with me—it's her place. But I can't take water in front of my friends. Next time try using a little softer approach."

"Would it have worked?"

"No," he said with a heavy shake of his head. "But it might save you a cracked head sometime."

"Get some broth, Earl," Liv shouted, "and quit your bragging. You, boy! Haven't you gone yet?"

The doctor was a pudgy little man with a greasy

face and the whitest hands I'd ever seen. He had a napkin in his collar and I could smell pork roast.

"Yes."

"We need you, doc. Got a little girl bad sick."

"I'm eating."

"I know you're eating. This is important." He was reluctant still until I flashed one of those gold pieces DeLong had given me.

"Just let me get my bag."

He snatched it up quick, struggling into his coat as we walked hurriedly down the steps and into the alley.

I followed him back to the saloon, entering by the side door which led directly into the hotel portion of the building. Just as we turned into the alleyway, I caught, for a fraction of a second in the feeble light, a familiar face. Or at least I thought it was familiar.

"What's the matter?"

"Nothing. Let's go in." I looked once more into the shadows by the rain barrel, but there was no one there, and I had no time to investigate then.

"In here, Doc," Liv said, holding open the door. "You, stay out," she said, pushing me back firmly. "You'd be of no help now."

Polecat was still squatting near the door, apparently not moving since I had left. I walked back to the alley door, opened it, and peered out. It was all dark silence, except for a yapping dog somewhere down near the wharfs. The fog was still thicker, filling the spaces between the buildings with cottony gray.

"What is it?"

"I don't know, Polecat. A face. Someone I might have known. Maybe someone who reminded me of someone."

That must have been it. My mind must have been playing tricks on me with the nervous excitement, the fog which warped distance and perspective.

"Who was it? Who did you think you saw, Clay?"

"A man called Jake."

A man called Jake who had been with the killers of my father and then with my own ambushers. A man I left for dead in Montana. Here in Oregon? Why, if it was actually Jake and not some illusion spun by the fog and the night?

"Boy!" It was the doctor, his finger beckoning me.

"Yes." He was standing there, competent-looking, his face expressionless with the open door behind him.

"She'll be all right. At least I believe so. But she can't be moved. Not for now." I must have looked worried.

"That's all right," Liv said. "She can stay here as long as necessary. I'll take my belongings to another room."

"That's kind of you," I remarked, and I meant it. What was it about this woman's eyes that caught mine and held them?

I waited with Polecat while Liv packed a few things and transported them to the room across the hall. Then for a moment we went in and stood by Wind on the Waters. The girl lay on her back, her hair patted back off her damp forehead, looking pale and small and frail. Her dark eyes flickered open once and the edges of her mouth turned up in a vain attempt at a smile.

"I think she will get well now," Polecat guessed.

"We didn't watch her closely enough. I should have seen it coming on." It was true. I had been so obsessed with getting to Oregon, with my revenge, that the girl had been the furthest thing from my thoughts. Now, seeing her there, peacefully asleep, her eyelids fluttering, her hands folded on the sheets like two soft doves, I wondered how I could have been so insensitive.

"That's enough, men," Liv said.

She had taken her hair down, and it fell across her shoulders. She had a green satin ribbon against the red of her hair. Her light blue eyes no longer seemed hard, or purposeful even, but simply weary.

We went out and Liv shut the door quietly after one last look at Wind on the Waters, leaving the lamp turned low on the bureau.

"Thanks," I said. She had begun to walk away toward her own room and she stopped as I spoke, turning her head back.

"It's nothing at all," Liv said. "What are kinfolk for if not to help out?"

TEN

We stood in the dark hallway, searching each other's faces. Liv was past her prime, but a fine-looking woman under the powder, and her eyes had an undaunted gleam in them. She smiled quickly once again and something clicked within me, dimly, nagging at my memory.

"Kinfolk. You said kinfolk?"

"That's right, Clayborne. Your mother was my sister. I'm Liv Thatcher. Don't look at me like that. I'd know you anywhere. You've got the strong look of your father. Just looking at you . . . it takes me back nearly twenty years to when that young plainsman came trooping into town with his buckskins and his cool eyes. . . . I took to him right off."

"But Sarah. My sister. Your mama." Her eyes grew wistful, lost in memories. "Sarah was shy and she turned her face from the bold mountain man. So naturally," she said with a weak smile, "your daddy took a notion for her. He was a man who liked his country wild and his women gentle. I never was a gentle sort, Clayborne."

"Clay."

"All right. Clay. It suits you better."

"Will you tell me about it? I mean. . . . I never knew my mother. Not really. Except that Pa set great store by her. There was always an empty spot left inside him that I couldn't fill. It was my mother's love he was aching for."

"I'll tell you." She said it somewhat harshly, and it surprised me. "If you'll tell me what brought you here."

"Go," Polecat said. He was a man who understood these things. "I'll wait outside Wind on the Waters's door. If she is troubled, I'll call you." He nodded again. "Go," he said warmly.

Liv let me into the small room. It was musty, empty-smelling, not like the warm room where we had left the Indian girl. On the floor in the corner was a saddle collecting dust, left, I supposed, by a cowboy who had left town in a big hurry.

I sat down on the bed at her request and watched as she lighted a cigar, something I had never seen a woman do, or even imagined a woman doing. She drew her wrap tighter around her and rubbed her arm. Then she nervously fingered her hair, shrugging an excuse for the cigar.

"A habit picked up from being too much around men," she apologized.

"My father's dead." I waited for that to soak in, but she must have guessed as much. She smiled weakly as if to say, "I'm sorry," and I went on, telling her the whole story, including my suspicions of her brother's part in the affair.

"It's possible," Liv said quietly. "Nate never did like your father. I recall the first night he came to supper, Sarah nervous and trembling as a rabbit, but proud of this tall young fellow of hers. Nate sniffed and walked out of the room. We came up from Virginia, you know. And your father . . ."

"Fought for the Union during the war."

"Yes," she nodded. "And this was soon after the war, Clay. Too soon. There were painful memories. Our home had been burned, our father killed at Chancellorsville. But there was more to it than that. More than this hate the southerner nurtured against the Yankee."

"What?"

"I don't know," she said, blowing smoke out. "But I had the feeling that they had met before. Perhaps before the war, or even during it.

"Nate was a lieutenant colonel during the war—he rose quickly through the ranks. Very quickly," she went on. "There were a number of points concerning his wartime service about which my brother was quite vague. I know he came west of the Mississippi at one time—to Colorado—and although he was in the Confederate Army, he wore no uniform at that time."

"To Colorado."

"Is that important?"

"Yes. My father was going back there when he was murdered. Where is your brother now?"

"Who knows?" she shrugged. "He was said to be sailing for Alaska—the fur trade is a prosperous business still. But he often sails in secret and returns with the holds of his ship still empty, his coffers full of gold."

"Surely his family . . ."

"Maybe his brothers know. Miles surely must know something. He is a trader, after all, with three ships in the China trade. Jay may know something as well, but I doubt it. He drinks too much. Nate would hardly tell him anything he wished kept secret. No," she said, "whatever Captain Thatcher's secrets are, he keeps them well."

"You . . ."

"I know nothing more, Clay," Liv told me, stubbing out her cigar in a saucer. "Nor do I wish to. He is my brother, but I have no interest in his life, his property, or his sins."

When I went out Polecat was gone. I peered into the room where Wind on the Waters lay. She was quiet, breathing softly, so I closed it again and crept out. I was suddenly aware of a gnawing hunger.

The saloon was filled to overflowing with drunken sailors and trappers. Smoke hung heavy in the air. Curses and arguing voices competed with the banging of a tinny piano.

"How's chances of getting a bite?" I asked Earl.

"Closed down the kitchen. You'll have to try the Chanty. Down on the corner of B Street and Posthill Road, near on to the wharfs."

I tried to talk to him some more, but the saloon was a faintly suppressed pandemonium. I eased out past a couple of rough-looking, raw-smelling sailors. One of them, in striped shirt and stocking cap, watched me closely, his sunken black eyes both vicious and amused.

B Street was little more than an alley with frequent, deep chuckholes filled with water from a recent rain. A yowling cat scurried around the corner in front of me, overhead the palest of half moons peered into the alleyway.

Houses jutted out over the street, and it was difficult to tell if they were empty or just unusually quiet. A man with a nasty limp came by me and stared when he lifted his eyes.

"Know where Posthill Road is?"

"Posthill? No. I don't know, mister." He pushed

past me and as he did I caught a worried—frightened?—expression on his toothless face.

There was a break in the houses where another street intersected it, and it was there that they jumped me.

Two of them came off from the left and another from my right. I took the first thug by the shoulders and rolled him over my knee and to the alley where he landed with a grunt.

"You'll pay for that," he muttered, but he said it with only half his wind. I had already turned to his partners. One of them was a giant of a man and he swung down hard with something heavy, a table leg maybe, taking me on the shoulder.

It drove me to my knees and my shoulder filled with fiery pain, but I had enough sense to move aside quickly and a second, driving blow whished harmlessly past my ear. It was my turn.

I came up with a solid right to the wind and the man doubled over. As he did I lifted my knee as hard as possible and turned to the third man. In his hand a knife glinted.

He waved it at me, but I didn't wait for him to get set. I kicked hard at his kneecap and caught it. He grunted, stepped back and tried to run, but I had him by the throat, cutting off his wind. The knife fell to the alley and I brought my forearm up hard against his chin, bringing a gush of blood from his mouth.

"He was supposed to be a kid," I heard one of them complain. It was the big man and he circled in slowly, the table leg, club, or whatever it was held cocked back.

He lunged and I stepped aside, tripping him, grabbing at the club, but he was too strong. The other man was off the ground. I recognized him now as the sailor in the striped shirt I had passed in the saloon. He dug into his belt and came up with a billy club. I stepped back, threw a hard left at the big man, kicked out again at the man with the knife, and tried to wiggle free.

And then they were all over me, their bodies close, heavy. I could feel the heat from them, smell liquor and sweat on their bodies. My arms were pinned back, but I managed to jerk my left free and get a good shot into the face of the man in the striped shirt, splitting his cheek. But the fat man's club flashed in the moonlight and came down hard on my neck. Then it fell again and it hit my skull with a dazing, sickening thump. I went down, still swinging my fists, but they hit nothing and the world went black, spinning crazily by as the wetness spread.

When I awakened it was wetter still. My head throbbed like a hammer on an anvil. I didn't move. I could hear voices and other faint sounds, but I couldn't sort them out just then. Wherever I was, whoever they were, I didn't want them to know I was conscious just yet.

Gradually it came to me. There was a steady swelling motion and the air smelled of salt. Oars worked in the oarlocks of the small boat and I could make out the legs of my two captors. The man in the striped shirt sat in the bow, beyond him the sky was a mat of stars. The big man had gone. Probably he was a professional bully boy hired for the job. What job? I was being shanghaied and there was nothing for it.

"Very profitable, Scully," the little man said.

Scully, the man in the striped shirt, smiled but there was no humor in it. "Who'd a thought the kid would have that much gold on him."

"The Captain might ask about it."

"He won't. What's he care as long as the kid's gone? He's got all he needs anyway," Scully growled.

So they had found the gold Yule DeLong had given me. In my boot I had stashed away one double eagle, but no matter. Where I was going it would be a long time before I spent it. The bottom of the boat was seeping badly and I was soaked. Still I kept down. I was sure they would be ready for me this time.

"I'd hate to be on board the *Scylla* myself," Scully said. "Captain Orduna is as bad as Nate Thatcher himself."

"Orduna!" the other spat. "Boiled pig meat! That's what I think of him. Boiled pig meat."

So the skipper's name was Orduna, and the ship the *Scylla*. She was a black-hulled barkantine, low in the water as she rode at anchor. Her square-rigged foremast was already carrying sail in the moderate breeze. The *Scylla* tugged at her tether. It would not be long before we were underway to . . . God knew where.

"Ho, the *Scylla*!"

The little man hailed her, standing, his hands cupped around his mouth. It was then or never and I came up, throwing all of my weight to one side of the skiff and she rolled, flipping the man overboard where he floundered and cursed, gurgling.

I dove toward the black skin of the water, fighting back Scully but the sailor was waiting for me when I came up, clubbing viciously at me with an oar. I went under, fighting the water, the pain and the cutting blows overhead.

I came up farther away from the *Scylla*, but not far enough. From somewhere another boat had appeared with four salty-looking seamen in it and two of them came into the water, throwing me back onto the boat choking, gasping. A trickle of blood came from my forehead where the oar had caught me flush.

"Come along, laddy. Come along. It ain't so bad once ye get yer sea legs." The speaker was a plump man with florid cheeks and chin whiskers. He puffed amiably on a pipe and nodded as two of the sailors sat on my legs, pinning me down.

"You'll tell Thatcher we brung him!" Scully yelled from the other boat.

"Be damned! You'd a lost him sure," the man with the whiskers yelled. "Tell Thatcher when you see him that Boots McCafferty took the lad."

"Hope the sea swallows you, McCafferty! And be damned!" Scully yelled back, following that with a torrent of curses.

"He'll get over that," McCafferty laughed.

"He will," I said through the pain. "They've got two hundred dollars off me. He's laughing right now."

I met Orduna as they pulled me on board the *Scylla*. He wasted no time. A cruel, hollow-eyed man, fleshy but without color he stepped to me and slashed my face with his fist.

"Yer on my ship and I'm to be your captain, do yer understand?"

"I understand." His eyes were hard on me. A trickle of blood was running from the corner of my mouth. McCafferty was holding me back by the collar of my coat.

"Good. See yer do. Or I'll feed you to the there-below. Let 'em grind yer bones." His mouth twisted into a mockery of a smile and then he turned and walked a step away. With his back to me he added, "I've been paid to keep yer off the beach—there's many a way to do it if yer find yer don't like the life of a shipee."

"Get shed of those clothes, laddie," McCafferty said as the captain went out of earshot. "You'll likely do no hunting on board the *Scylla*." He nodded toward my moccasins and buckskins.

"Likely not." He saw me watching the skipper.

"Don't get ideas, laddie. Enjoy the sailing. He's a dozen men could break you in two like a dry twig."

"And you? Are you one of them?"

"Get shed of the clothes."

Aft of the wheelhouse McCafferty showed me the way below decks. They let me go down by myself, and I knew I had bought it for the time being. We were more than a mile to sea, the water high, gray, and choppy. I was not that kind of a swimmer. Already the anchor was being reeled up, the creaking of the capstan overhead told me that much. We would soon be under way—and I did not even know where we were bound.

I worked along the dark gangway making for the crew's quarters—a large, stale room lit feebly by a dangling lantern, the hammocks hung in tiers of five along the curve of the hull. A rat scrabbled off across the dark floor and the ship canted over hard to port, apparently catching the wind, setting her course. A small sound caught my ear and I turned to find a pair of animal eyes watching from the dark corner. But they belonged to a man, not an animal.

"I need some sailor's clothes."

The eyes did not waver. They were small, dark eyes belonging to a hunched, narrow ape of a man. His hands folded across his lap, palms up. He was naked to the waist and filthy.

"Where is the *Scylla* bound? Do you know?"

"Don't bother," a voice interrupted. A burly mate came in through the door, dug through a duffle bag, and tossed some clothes at me. "Old Gaelyn, he's had a touch too much of the sea." He tapped his head. "Crazy, I mean. Drank a gallon of sea water from the bilge a few days ago."

"But why?"

"Who knows," the mate shrugged. "Crazy, I told you. Hardly a man anymore, is he?" He looked at the withered Gaelyn and spat on the floor. "You get dressed! We've need of hands right now—voluntary or not."

Gaelyn watched the mate leave, his eyes frightened, bright. Then he watched me dress, his eyes sweeping up and down my frame.

"Shanghaied . . ."

It was a tiny, cracked voice, barely human.

"Yes. I was shanghaied. My uncle arranged it," I said with a faint smile.

"I'm . . . shanghaied," Gaelyn said quietly, watching his hands which rested inertly on his lap.

"We'll get off," I promised him. He shook his head.

"We'll get off," I said again, going nearer. Suddenly those hands which seemed dead flashed out with incredible swiftness and took my wrists. I tried to shake off but couldn't. Gaelyn's eyes were fixed on mine.

"You'll take me off!"

Gaelyn dug his fingers even tighter into my wrists. His grip was steel, impossibly strong considering his emaciated appearance.

"I said I would."

"You'll get me off . . ." Gaelyn whimpered. "Five . . ."

Without warning a big, meaty hand flashed in front of my eyes. The mate had returned and his fist caught Gaelyn flush on the cheek, sending him scurrying to another corner like a whipped cur.

"Don't get him stirred up," the mate hissed. "We'll have to get rid of him if he gets worked up again. You're doing him no favor."

"He said . . ."

"He said he was shanghaied." The mate shrugged.

"He said something else. I'm not sure. I thought he said five years!"

"Five years below decks. Yes," the mate replied maliciously. "Didn't you see? Look closely."

I did and saw them—shackles around his legs, with scars, deep purple scars on his ankles where they had rubbed, healed and been torn open again. Those chains had been on there for years. I turned away from the pitiful man-beast.

"You see how it is." The mate threw back his head and laughed harshly. An ugly man with tattoos snaking up each thick, hairy arm, he scowled, cuffed my ear, and shoved me toward the hatch.

"Get topside! You want to end up like this, you can."

"What kind of a ship is this? Devil ship! Hell ship! Slave ship!"

"Yes. All those, and more perhaps. Now get a move on! Unless you wish to become like Gaelyn Orduna."

"Orduna!"

"Aye. He's the captain's brother, boy. His own flesh and blood. Now do you think he'll be more kindly toward you?" Again the mate laughed, a booming horrible laugh that rattled around inside the bowels of the *Scylla* and died there like a hellish curse.

ELEVEN

———◆———

There had been conjecture that we were Alaska bound, along that golden-and-white coast where the Indians rowed out to meet the traders, their canoes filled with rich, valuable furs of mink and otter, seal and ermine, begging to trade for steel and flint, wool coats and blankets; but the *Scylla* turned her bow southward.

The ship's sails filled with wind and mushroomed out, her sleek black hull skimming over the placid blue waters as we traveled south, ever southward, the cliffs along the coast always in sight, always out of reach.

I kept to myself and did as I was told without complaining. Orduna's eyes were on me—as I knew they would be—and those of the big first mate whose name, I learned, was Coombs.

Coombs stopped me at my work the third day out. "Learning to like it, are you?" he asked with a heavy leer.

"I'll like it. I like it better than shackles," I told him. That satisfied him and he grunted, walking off across the easy rolling deck.

I was growing to like the snap of the sails in the fresh breeze, the pelicans and gulls following in our wake, the calm, starlit nights, but I had no idea of giving up my escape attempts. I would bide my time and the opportunity would come. A ship must put to port for water, for whatever commerce it engaged in; when it did I would be ready. And perhaps I would take one other man with me—I had given a promise to Gaelyn Orduna.

"You're a silent one," Boots McCafferty said. The sun was hot, and the whiskered, cheerful man puffed his pipe as we worked bare-chested splicing ropes.

"It does me no good to spout off."

"Canny. You've learned something already," he nodded with an agreeable smile. "Leave me show you something with that weave," he said, taking the rope from my hands.

With amazing skill and deftness he unraveled my splice and separated the strands, weaving them again with tight spacings. His hands were thick, broken-knuckled, but you'd never know it to watch McCafferty's work.

"Man and boy I been a sailor," he told me, as I watched him work. "The sea is my wilderness, my peaceful refuge. On the land there are towns filled with iniquity, a snare at every juncture. But here," he said, swinging his stubby arm in a wide arc, "what is there to confine a man?"

"Shackles," I told him. I took up the finished rope and stowed it away.

"It ain't so bad, boy," McCafferty told me, speaking quietly as I coiled the rope into the locker.

"You're a free man," I replied. "It's not bad for you. But for me . . . or for Gaelyn."

He frowned, scratching at his white whiskers. Then he shook his head. "I was shanghaied my first time out. Came to love it. The sea will be my winding sheet, and never a more beautiful silken shroud could there be."

"Many a prison's a beautiful place," I said. "For me the sea's a cage, broad though she is. This ship's a cell, and you—though I favor you McCafferty—are a jailer."

I understood how he felt, but not why he sailed such a ship. I watched the waters pass, the faraway coastline slither by, and I yearned to touch it, to smell the piney woods, the cedar, and clover of the high country, to walk the game trails on the high, purple mountains. I yearned for it, for my Montana. And I worried.

There was a young Indian girl back in Oregon, lying sick still for all I knew. A girl who had no one and knew nothing of the white world. Thank God she was with Liv Thatcher. The woman was rough, but a good one. And Wind on the Waters had Polecat nearby. Yet what help could he be?

He could protect her, but the Piegan had no more of an idea how to survive in this new world than she did. They could not go back to their home, not with Quail Walker alive to stir up memories of Yellow Glove's death. A death caused by the girl's disregard for her tribal vows.

I lay in my swaying hammock at night below decks and thought of her cheery, grave face. And by day I watched the wandering sea, feeling and seeing the wind on the waters of this vast ocean.

On the sixteenth day we closed for port.

The coastline was a low, sandy stretch of beach with raw, bare mountains jutting up in the distance. There were several palm-thatched huts on the beach and one fishing boat that I saw. I had been told that this village was Puerto La Paloma—the first fragment of Mexican soil I had seen. It fascinated me and with its aspect, so different from my home country woods and grasslands, it called up the urge to explore, to walk the harsh, cactus-studded badlands beyond the beach.

It was an urge that would be fulfilled, more . . . sated.

The anchor was cast when we were still a good thousand yards off the coast, and the boat put down. Orduna and three of his crew got into it and pulled for shore as we watched.

"Get no ideas," Coombs breathed into my ear as I stood at the rail. "There's sharks in those pearly waters. And muskets at your back."

Orduna was met on the beach by a party of men. I could make out little of it, but the men seemed to be dignitaries, wearing sashes of red ribbon and plumed hats.

The work party was setting-to now, taking the second boat, the larger one for water, using tackle to lower the hundred-gallon oak barrels the *Scylla* used to store her sweet water.

Boots McCafferty came up beside me, his constant pipe in his jaws. I nodded to the activity on the beach.

"What's that?"

"Party of the locals. General Hector Cedeno."

"What's our business with him?"

"Yours? You have no business with him." McCafferty wagged his head, almost worriedly. I could see he didn't want to discuss it, but if I was to have any hope of getting free I had first of all to know the ropes.

"I thought the *Scylla* was a trader in furs."

"At times. At times your uncle has dealt with fur traders. At other times not." McCafferty looked around once and then added, "This time it's a more profitable trade he's looking to make."

"With Cedeno? He's a soldier? What could he have to fill our holds?"

"You're too curious, lad."

"I'll find out in time. Besides, who could I tell?"

"It's true," McCafferty allowed. "It's opium, son. The *Scylla*'s running opium."

"Opium . . . for where?"

"San Francisco."

"The Chinese trade?"

"Some of it. Some of it. But the Chinese usually take care of their own trade, bringing it in from the old country themselves with couriers—poor men who buy their passage by making such deals.

"During the late war, Clay, a great many men were in a great deal of pain. Rebel and Yankee alike. Legs torn free, amputations made without even corn liquor to kill the pain . . . horrible wounds made by grapeshot and cannon balls. But we had a gift from the gods—or so it seemed then, a gift which could kill the gnawing, horrible pain and let a man sleep with it."

"Morphine."

"That's right. Morphine. But morphine has a second face beside that angel of mercy's face it showed the suffering soldier. A devil's face it is, Clay."

"It's addictive."

"Aye. Addictive—that's hardly the word! I've seen men cling to morphine gratefully for the pain, and when the pain is gone try to tear the beast from them. It's a tenacious poison, it demands, it sucks at a man's mind and conscience. It's a rotting, killing substance."

"So my Uncle Nate uses this ship for transporting

opium to be made into morphine—preying on other men's illnesses."

"Aye. This ship and three others. And your Uncle Miles delivers it after they've produced morphine from it. And this Cedeno, he brings the contraband out of the interior. Some of it is packed over the mountains by mule or backpack from Guatemala and even farther south. This is the way he serves in his Army! It's a foul nest, Clay."

I looked deeply into McCafferty's eyes. He knew my question—why was he here if the business disgusted him? He opened his mouth as if to speak, but turned instead and walked away. Maybe he had no answer to give me.

It was midnight before Orduna returned, the oars of his boat lapping gently at the water. Earlier there had been torches on the shore, the sounds of music and revelry. Cedeno must have been pleased with the sale.

I lay in my hammock listening until it was quiet, with only the sea sounds to break the utter stillness, then I rose and quietly slipped into the dark bowels of the main hold. There was a sailor at the watch, but he snored quietly, his head drooped forward. I clubbed him with a billy just below the ear, and he slumped forward into a deeper sleep. He would never know what had happened, but he would awake with a powerful headache.

The chest was in the far corner. Bound with brass bands and locked twice, it was solid enough. Looking around, I found a piece of strap iron which seemed stout enough for the job.

I slid it under the clasps and strained. Nothing. I looked around, but there was only the swaying of the ship, the shadows dancing from the swinging lantern at the far end of the musty hold. The clasp gave. And then the other and inside there were packed five dozen brick-sized, oilskin-wrapped bundles. The sweat was raining from my forehead, and suddenly I felt that I was as crazy as Gaelyn for doing this. They would kill me if I were caught, and even if I managed to escape where could I go?

I took the iron strap and punctured the opium packets, brick by brick. Then I threw them to the floor of the hold where the white powder scattered like a heavy dust. The easiest place to knock a hole in her was just overhead where a knothole butted against a flimsy patch made by an inexperienced shipwright. I took up a mallet and hit against it with all my strength. The mallet made a heavy echo in the stillness of the hold. I caught my breath and hit it again, bringing a small trickle of sea water from the seam. Again I hit, and again the sound of the falling mallet seemed to roar in the hull.

I drove my mallet at it again and the knot fell loose. In seconds a stream of water was gurgling into the hold. I broke for the hatch as the opium underfoot was devoured by the sea.

I had one foot on the ladder when a burly sailor appeared at the head of it, musket in hand.

"Jones?"

"Aye!" I replied. He bent lower to look closely and my hand shot out, taking his musket barrel. He toppled headlong past me, hitting the wet floor with a splash and a muffled curse.

I kept the musket to hand and scrambled up the ladder to the fore deck where the sea and sky offered a deceptively serene picture, the stars brilliant and silver in the black sky.

"Hey there!" the helmsman called, coming from the wheel.

"What's the trouble?"

"You! What're you doing a-deck?"

"Cap'n sent me. Says we've sprung a join below decks."

"What? What's that?"

He came to me and I produced the musket. He threw up his hands and began backing toward the rail, his face paralyzed with fear. "I've got a wife," he mumbled.

"Tell her hello," I said. I jabbed him once with the musket as he backed to the rail and he tumbled backward into the black waters. Hurriedly, I rushed aft again and down the gangway.

"Gaelyn!"

His black eyes turned up, his face smiling stupidly. "You're taking me?"

"I am. Move quickly now."

He came after me, the muffled clank of his chains rattling against the deck.

"Help me with the boat."

It was still quiet, but there was a list to the ship and an unhealthy growling in her depths. The water was building up. Gaelyn worked merrily at the boat, lowering it with a beaming smile. I leaped for her as she hit the waters, free.

On board tumult erupted suddenly. There were voices cursing and screams, then lanterns were lit. Above us Coombs appeared, a rifle in his hands, an ugly scowl on his fat face.

"Hold to, boy! Hold to or you're dead!"

Before I could react a stubby figure of a man appeared behind Coombs, and the mate jerked and fell into the water, the man behind him standing hesitantly with his rifle.

"Jump, McCafferty! Jump!"

Boots McCafferty looked behind him where men rushed past in confusion, then down at where he had thrown the first mate and he leaped, feet first toward our skiff where Gaelyn sat jubilantly clapping his hands together.

I helped McCafferty on board and then we three were alone on the wide and empty sea. A boy, a mutineer, and a crazy man. And behind us we had left the *Scylla*, now tilted crazily to port, filled with antlike sailors and lantern light. And before us—a land none of us knew. A fearful, desert land where we had little hope of survival and an entire army waiting to prevent us from reaching the authorities with our tale.

McCafferty was silent, and no wonder. I tugged steadily on my oars, watching the diminishing bulk of the *Scylla*. Only Gaelyn could laugh about our situation and feel joyous about it . . . and he, of course, was insane.

TWELVE

◆●◆

It was still dark as we beached the boat beneath the rust-brown cliffs north of Puerto La Paloma, but within an hour the sun would already be scraping its way above the horizon, tinting the long white runners of surf foam a faint pink.

"Get the boat ashore. We'll find a place to hide it."

"Scuttle her," McCafferty said. His face was anguished panic.

"We may need it," I said. "We may not get the chance, but we may need the boat."

"You'd row up the coast?"

"Rather than face an army ashore, I would."

Gaelyn was still sitting in the prow, dreamily watching the black figure of the *Scylla* offshore. We had to pull him from the boat, but we got it ashore and hid it in a tiny cove, draping some kelp over her to conceal her further.

"Now what?"

"I don't know." McCafferty's hound eyes were on me. He was fumbling for a match though his pipe had gone in the drink.

"We'll find a way out."

"You'd better, boy. I must've been crazy. Why did I do it!" he moaned, holding his head.

"Because it was right, Boots. Coombs would have

killed us. Now get yourself together. We're in for a run if not for a fight."

"You're right. Well," he said, "we've the rifle."

It was a Jaeger rifle, caliber fifty, and a fine piece in its day. Yet I wondered how it would do against repeaters. Perhaps in the village we could find another weapon or two. I suggested this to McCafferty.

"I don't think it's wise. Nor do I favor using the boat again. The *Scylla* has two twelve-pound cannon astern, and she'd blow us merrily from the water."

"You may be right. Then we have no choice. It's up the beach and then inland as soon as possible. Because Cedeno will undoubtedly be on our scent."

"Aye!" McCafferty was calmer now. "I'm thinking we'll need horses . . . but that too means the village."

"Linea del Cielo."

The voice was soft and it was a moment before we realized that Gaelyn had spoken.

"Linea del Cielo," the man said again. "High up. On the skyline . . . Linea del Cielo."

"Yes. Yes, what about it?" McCafferty asked impatiently.

"I was there before. I have friends, you bet."

"Where is this place, Gaelyn," I asked, taking him by the shoulders. His hand went up and his bony finger pointed beyond the cliffs and into the interior where the jagged, barren mountains the color of dust scraped the belly of the sky.

"We can't go on what he says."

"Why not? He's been here before, Boots. Neither of us knows a single man. I think we should risk it. At least we may find horses there. Are you sure, Gaelyn?" I asked again, and again his finger pointed to the mountains.

"Good hombre. Pedro y Alejandro. *Muy bueno, Amigos para* Gaelyn . . . *si*! Linea del Cielo. Pedro *es un aguila descalza.*"

I glanced at McCafferty amazed at Gaelyn's spate of Spanish. "What's he say? Do you know?"

"Aye. There's two friends of his there, at Linea del Cielo. Good men. Pedro, so he says, is a man who knows just what he's up to."

"I hope we do, Boots. I hope we do. But I think we'd better put our trust in Gaelyn this time. What else can we do?"

We climbed to the top of the cliffs, reaching the flat desert beyond as the sun thrust its fiery saber through the notches in the broad, sawtooth range beyond. Color bled out across the barren land, the only shadows cast by thick clumps of cholla—jumping cactus and those mysterious, shaggy plants called boojum.

An hour we struggled forward, moving silently with only the swishing sounds our pant legs made, turning our heads back frequently, watching for the long rank of horsemen to appear—and none of us had a doubt they would appear.

General Hector Cedeno was a smuggler, a drug trafficker, a man lining his own pockets at government expense. He would not allow us freely out of the country. And Orduna would be spurring him on, furious at the loss of the opium and our escape.

"Hot." McCafferty mumbled it, but it was in all our minds. Hot was no word for it. The sweat rained from us, soaking our shirts, the furnace winds blasted us dry and peppered us with sand. Underfoot the sand, so deep that we sank to our calves, was a frying pan. We trudged onward, the mountains receding before us. At first they had seemed no more than ten miles off in the absolutely clear atmosphere, unclouded by fog or smoke, but now I knew they were a good deal farther, twice as far at least.

"Them mountains have legs," McCafferty swore. His footwear was already coming apart. We all had huge blisters developing, and we didn't dare remove our boots, for the swelling would prevent us from getting them back on. There was the heat.

The sun had gone to a brilliant white ball, fiercely defending the sky from prying eyes like some jealous father. The desert flats were white, giving off shimmering veils of rising heat. The ground in these playas was cracked, brittle for mile upon mile. It was here that the waters collected and evaporated again . . . when there was water, and there was none.

"I'm dying for a drink. Dying for it," McCafferty said. His voice was strangely cracked, small. Only Gaelyn went on cheerfully, though his lips were already blistered, his eyes sunburned red.

"There's water. There's water." He mumbled as he moved across the playa, his stork legs chewing up the miles.

At midmorning we could take it no longer. The sun was boiling our brains. My head throbbed horribly, my skin was dry and chalky. We found scant shade under a leafless, spiny plant called mesquite. Gaelyn insisted the beans were edible, but I found them bitter, alumlike.

"Horses eat them," the madman said. He went off wandering in the sun, his shirt tied over his head as Boots and I sat perspiring, dust-caked, in the woven shade of the slender mesquite.

"We're crazier than he is," Boots panted. "Follow-

ing a madman across the desert. What sort of godfor-
saken country is this!" he screamed, his upraised
hands clenched into bitter fists.

"Where else would we go?" It was difficult to speak,
my tongue was swollen, my mouth dry as the sand.
"He seems to know the way. He says there's water," I
managed to say.

"He seems to know—he thinks it's a cool day! He
thinks these blasted seeds are bon-bons!" Boots scattered a handful of sand then leaped to his feet.

Not three feet away from us a nearly white rat-
tlesnake had been lying in the sand, buried to its protruding eyes. McCafferty's sand flinging had stirred it
and it slithered toward us with amazing quickness in
a curious end for end motion.

"Sidewinder!" McCafferty hollered. "Get back!"

There was no need to call out. I danced away like I
had a hot foot. The sidewinder, ornery by nature,
had been disturbed taking a nap in the shade. They
say the sidewinder is the only rattler that'll run at a
man, and that may or may not be so, but this one
sure bluffed us out from under that mesquite.

Gaelyn came in walking just as we had abandoned
the shade to the snake. He smiled and nodded.

"His chin's wet!" McCafferty shouted. And it surely
was. "He's been drinking water! Sweet water."

"Sure. There's good water," Gaelyn said. "But you
got to look close."

"You tell us where or I'll strangle your skinny
neck," McCafferty said. The sun was getting to the
sailor, that much was obvious. Gently I removed his
hands from Gaelyn's throat.

"Where's the water, Gaelyn?" I asked him.

"Right there. Just by the big rocks. You'll see. There's a patch of grass to mark it."

McCafferty was off, nearly running. When I found him he was on his belly, sucking the water from a tiny bowl in a large rock down the wash. I waited until he was through, and then I drank. I drank more than I thought a man could, soaking my hair and clothing when I was finished.

Side by side, McCafferty and I lay on the dry grass, letting the water fill each deprived cell of our heat-battered bodies. We were like that when Gaelyn came to us, whistling.

"Thank you," I told him.

He cocked his head curiously, like a dog, and scratched his head, not understanding why I would thank him for water. He crouched down beside us, however, and whispered softly. "Soldiers. I seen 'em just now. A lot of soldiers, Clay. I think they want to kill us."

From the top of the low dune I could see them, strung out across the desert like avenging angels.

"We can get a couple of them," McCafferty said. He had the rifle in his hands.

"Better we keep moving. They don't seem to be sure of our tracks—the sand is soft, and the tracks could be old or new, ours or anyone else's. If we fire all we'll be doing is giving them our location precisely."

"I don't have any running left in me."

"Then you'll have to stay and talk to them, Boots. I can't carry you. Come on," I said, clasping his shoulder, "a man doesn't know what he can do until he's tried, and we sure enough got reason for trying."

"All right," he nodded. "Let's go."

We dog trotted, keeping to the low ground, the washes, as we wove toward the mountains. The earth underfoot was rocky, jagged, and hot. McCafferty's eyes were glazed and he ran drunkenly, his face waxen.

I was the youngest, and used to walking or running. I had climbed mountains all of my life, and crossed them. But McCafferty was nearly fifty, a pudgy man used to hard work, but not to this. Gaelyn ran crazily along, sometimes ahead of me. He was thin, wiry, but it seemed that it was only an insane energy that prodded him forward.

McCafferty went down several times. The last time hard, his chin splitting open under the impact. He lay there a long while until we turned him over. Blood matted his wreath of white chin whiskers and his face was cool despite the heat.

"I can't make her. Let them shoot me, I'd rather."

"The sun will be down in an hour. It's cooling. Then we can slow down. They can't follow us in the dark."

"No. I want the sea. Let them take me to her."

"Orduna will have you in shackles—or worse."

"I don't care. I no longer care, Clay!"

"We'll make an attempt at carrying you."

"That's absurd."

"Lie there awhile. We'll wait awhile. You catch your breath."

"I can't! I can't breathe in this furnace box. I'm cut for the sea. To live there or to die there. Say I've done you a service, Clay, and let it go. If you try to carry me now, it'll only undo whatever I have done for you." He closed his eyes heavily, the lids puffy and red. He breathed in slowly through blistered, cracked lips.

"No. I can't leave you."

"I want to be left. Don't you see? What's for me in those damnable mountains? Barren wasteland—no, I'm for the sea. Let them drown me in it; I'll die happy."

There was no more time to talk of it. I could hear horses nickering not far away. We could not carry him, not against his will. And I believed he really did wish to go back and throw himself on Orduna's mercy. "Will you keep the rifle, Boots?"

"No," he panted, lifting a hand. "Keep it. I'll not be fighting. Now go! Damn you, Clay, go! I don't want to see you caught."

He had begun to shiver and his eyes were positively black and distant. Suddenly it came to me. How could I have been so blind! I knew why Boots sailed the *Scylla,* and why he wanted to give himself up.

"Luck to you, Boots."

I put my hand on his square shoulder. He smiled weakly. He would be all right, at least I hoped so. He would have his morphine.

The way he had spoken of it, I should have guessed. His memory of the pain caused by it during the War between the States had seemed personal, immediate, and it was. Boots was a morphine addict himself, and the *Scylla* his home because it was there, and only there, that he could be certain of receiving a constant supply of the stuff.

"Luck to you, Boots McCafferty."

It must have cost him a great deal to jeopardize his position with Orduna, and I was grateful for it. But under any circumstances there was no way now to take Boots any farther. I nodded to Gaelyn, who sat nearby, in a monkey squat, and with one quick look back at Boots we began again, moving toward the far, forbidding mountains.

THIRTEEN

———◆———

Night came with a cooling rush, quickly on the wide and empty desert flats, streaking the flanks of the mountain peaks pink and golden, gilding the salt playas with deeper shades. The sun had no sooner gone down into the blushing sea than it became cold. Suddenly, nearly painfully so. By morning we would be in bad shape without shelter. Yet it beat shackles—I reminded myself of that constantly by looking at my miserable traveling companion.

I had time now to sort things out, and I tried to. I was worried about one thing—why was it that on that certain night, the night of our escape, I had found Gaelyn unchained? Could it be that we were being used? Was it possible? With Orduna, yes. But I could see no point in such a scheme.

I thought of the soldiers. It seemed odd that mounted men had not closed the gap as much as a hundred yards. And they had camped at sundown, building a fire. Where had they found firewood for that fire in this denuded land, unless they brought it with them? If that were the case, they would almost have had to be expecting this.

I shook off this tangle of suspicions and began working at my burning, swollen feet. The long tendons running to my toes were knotted up, and the balls of my feet covered with huge blisters. The cool air did some good. I hoped that the swelling would be gone by morning. Gaelyn sat solemnly nearby, taking no trouble to make himself comfortable.

"Gaelyn," I asked him, "when was it that you visited Linea del Cielo?"

"Not long ago. Some time."

"Why did you go there?"

"I don't know." He smiled again.

"Does the Captain—your brother—know of the place?" Gaelyn didn't answer, but no matter. If Orduna had not known of Linea del Cielo, by now they had gotten the information from Boots McCafferty. The general would surely know just where this place was.

I worried on that for a while before it came to me that it could make no difference. We were committed to that course now. Where else could we go? There was no place to run, no place to hide. I only hoped that Gaelyn's friends—if there were any such men—were at Linea del Cielo, and that they were as he had described them: Men who know what they're up to.

We crawled to our feet in the gray hours before dawn and as the sun burst over the scarred, ragged peaks of the mountains, we had already gone five miles. The ground was growing steeper now, littered with boulders washed from the mountains by flash floods, loosened by the winds. The cavalry was behind us still—a mile, perhaps, strung out in a loose file.

We struggled upward, in the shadow of the dust brown mountains, finding nothing for shade, nothing to drink or eat, just the scattered cholla and nopal, some barrel cactus, and an itinerant horned toad.

Gaelyn was short of breath now. My own lungs were fiery, my mouth dry as if filled with sand. The wind was an arid thrust at our backs, drying every drop of moisture as it formed. My feet, I was sure, were bleeding. I could feel the warm stickiness in my boots.

We stopped, leaning back against a great yellow boulder, panting. Gaelyn bent over, bracing his hands on his knees, sucking in great swallows of hot air. He pointed toward the mountain, trying to say something that did not come out in the dryness. But I knew what he meant. We had to climb.

The horsemen in a single rank moved across the desert. Black specters passing through the shimmer of heat waves, they seemed ghostly avengers. If we went now, into the mountains, we had a chance. No horse could be driven up the path we meant to take. It was our chance to gain some ground and so we started up.

It was midday, the sun hot on our backs, glaring off the rocks as we scrambled up, grabbing at rocks too hot to be grasped for long, tearing our flesh. And behind us the soldiers had started the climb. And they were fresh.

I could hear voices now. Muffled, but loud. They cursed as a hand came in contact with a frying pan hot rock or the man in front caused a trickle of rocks and dust to fall on his companion.

Gaelyn and I climbed madly. Two crazy men, it seemed, with but one thought. To keep on. To keep on until . . . what?

I did not know, but again the shackles came to mind, the burning eyes of Orduna, and the cat-o'-nine-tails which I had not seen, but heard a-plenty of.

Several times we started slides or tried to, but they were too small and we too weak for the rocks to be more than an inconvenience to our pursuers.

Still we climbed. My head spun with a dizzy headache. I felt disconnected from my body, a machine which climbed now of its own volition.

Then we found the trail. A narrow, sliver of a trail following the contours of the mountain. We dragged ourselves wearily to it and ran forward, along the sheer precipice, finally coming into the shade of a deep canyon. There was a dry watercourse where the infrequent rain rushed down over smooth white rocks, plummeting to the desert below. There the trail swung up and switched back.

Still we ran, until it seemed my entire life had been spent on the mountain, running. Until the trail dead-ended in a box with the lip of the canyon not more than twenty feet above us.

"There's no way up," I panted. "No way."

"We'll go," Gaelyn said. He was pale, pale as the sands, and bloody from head to ankles.

"All right," I nodded, panting it out. The soldiers were behind us. There was no way that a man could see, but by feeling with our fingers, testing every protruding stone before putting our weight on it, we were able to get nearly halfway up. I could hear footsteps on the trail behind us.

"Gaelyn!"

"No!" I'd come to a point where there was no purchase at all. No rock, no clump of grass to cling to, no crack to wedge my bleeding feet in.

"I can't . . ."

"No!" Gaelyn shouted again. For a moment I thought he might try to climb over me. "I'll throw myself off before I go back," he shouted. I glanced over my shoulder at the mountainside, falling away to desert nearly three thousand feet below. The wind ripped at my tenacious grip. My shirt hung in shreds, my fingers ached. And there we would be, targets hung on the wall for the soldiers when they came.

Then the big hand stretched down and jerked me up and over the rim of the cliff.

FOURTEEN

—◆—

"Buenas tardes, amigos." The Mexican who had pulled me up was a rugged-looking, narrow man with a cigar clenched in his teeth and a black sombrero dangling down his back. There were two others with him and one of them held his feet as he reached down once again and pulled Gaelyn up beside us.

"Esteban!"

The man who had been standing by nodded and stepped forward, unlimbering his Winchester. He fired a full magazine down into the canyon, and we could hear the soldiers cursing and dashing for cover. One of them, probably hit by a ricochet screamed out in pain. Esteban squatted on his heels and calmly reloaded his rifle.

"They will soon give up, I think."

"But after we leave . . ." I said, still finding my breath hard to catch. "They won't quit."

"They will have to," the tall man, the one with the cigar said.

"They may have a grappling hook."

"No. If they did—who will be the first man to come forward to see if we are truly gone?" He flashed a brilliant smile and nodded to Esteban, who again fired a volley of rifle shots.

"How did you find us?"

Gaelyn was still on the ground, his back rising and falling wretchedly as he struggled for breath.

"We watch always. We saw them yesterday and so we waited to see why they came. Usually it is for us they search. Usually they do not find us."

Gaelyn had turned over now and managed to sit up weakly. The tall man stepped back in surprise and shouted something in Spanish.

"Orduna," he said. "Gaelyn Orduna." He took Gaelyn's head and gave him tiny sips of water. "It is I. Pedro."

The three of them exchanged sharp, startled glances. Pedro gave Gaelyn water again and then looked at me.

"No wonder they followed you. But what has happened to Gaelyn?"

"His brother has had him prisoner. For years, I believe."

"A sin! Holy Mother, it is a sin. Such a fine strong man to have been broken like this. I did not recognize him. Alejandro! The horses, quickly!"

Carefully they helped Gaelyn onto a roan pony, tying his boots to the stirrups. All of the life had gone out of Gaelyn. He sagged and swayed in the saddle like a scarecrow.

Esteban stayed behind, crouched on the rim of the cliff. Now and then we heard a burst of rifle fire as we wove our way through the thick brush and stunted pinyon pine which passed for timber here.

"And you?" Pedro asked. "What have you to do with this?"

I told him my story as we rode toward a small village I could see already, nestled in the tiny valley beyond the stand of pinyon.

"I believe they may have let us escape," I said finally.

"It is likely. The mate's rifle may have been empty, or this McCafferty may have been motivated by different impulses than you believed. Perhaps Orduna ordered him to help you."

"I don't believe that. I can't. But why? It puzzles me."

"Gaelyn had been prisoner for a long time while his brother tried to extract certain information from him. And now, if what you say is so, Gaelyn can no longer speak coherently. Gaelyn could not tell his brother what he wanted to know, even under torture. But he could still lead him here."

"But why here?"

"You will see. It goes back a long while, Clay."

We had come into the small village. Adobe and tile, white in the late sunlight, it was a pretty setting against the higher mountains beyond. Chickens scratched in the street and a pair of black, slick dogs wrestled in the shade. A pantless boy streaked for home, his dirty face crying. There was clean wash hung out to dry and the soft, haunting strumming of a guitar somewhere. Yet there was something to mark Linea del Cielo as a different town than others of the same stamp across the Mexican countryside.

Here there was a man with a broad sombrero on the roof, a rifle in hand. Another watched from out of an alley. Three or four men loafed in front of a cantina, all of them draped with weapons and ammunition. Linea del Cielo was a fortress.

Pedro saw that I had noticed the guards.

"Yes. You will be safe here. You had better stay for a while. The opium you destroyed was not a part of Orduna's plan. For that he will kill you if he can."

We had come up before a small white house. There were already two horses at the rail. Pedro gave a shrill whistle and a man came out, wiping his hands on an apron. He looked at me questioningly and then at Gaelyn who appeared only half alive.

"Get him in, Raul. It's Gaelyn Orduna—and not in good shape. The sun was bad, the run too arduous."

A pretty dark-eyed girl had appeared beside her father. She watched me shyly, and I must have been quite a sight, dirty as I was, my torn shirt showing my shoulders through it, hatless, with a dirty shadow of beard.

"And my friend, Clay," Pedro said, "see that he is fed, Raul. I will pay."

"You will pay? Never, Pedro. Your money is no good here. I owe too much to you." The older man shook his head and turned to the girl. "Start the fire, Alicia. And air out the room in the back. These men will stay here for a while."

Raul took good care of us. First off they set up a table of tortillas, frijoles, beef with some of those hot yellow chili peppers, and some fresh fruit following to cool down the burning. While we leaned back, stuffed but still plenty dirty, the girl Alicia brought us coffee and some kind of candy made from the nopal cactus.

Gaelyn hadn't made a big dent in his serving, but he at least got some food in him. The coffee appealed to him more and he put away three or four cups. He had to steady his cup with both hands and his head hung weakly, but he too was looking better by the time we had finished.

It was growing to dark outside and the sky was pretty as a painter's pallette with rose-and-violet hues touched with gold. A party of men rode by the house slowly and I heard the guitar off in the near distance. Another girl came in, somewhat older than Alicia. She must've been near to my age, eighteen or so. Pretty, dark-eyed, proud, she wore a thin veil over her head and shoulders.

"My daughter, Alma," Raul said, and his eyes flashed with pride. No wonder. She was a jewel, and a lady. I understood she was engaged to Esteban, the man I had met on the cliff.

"Esteban has returned," Alma said, taking the veil off her head, though she left it draped on her shoulders as she ate daintily, following a brief prayer.

"These are the two men," Raul told her. "This one is Clay Rourke, the other Gaelyn Orduna."

"I am Alma," she said with a gracious nod. "Welcome to our home."

I couldn't get over the difference a few years could make in a girl. Alicia was cute as a fuzzy puppy, lithe and shy. But her sister was a woman, and a queenly one at that. Tall, straight in carriage, and I was sure one to conceal as a matter of course any displeasure or animosity.

Yet it was Alicia who caught my eye. She reminded me of another girl just that age I had met in the faraway hills . . . what had become of Wind on the Waters? Whatever happened to my plans to find the Thatcher brothers and repay them for what they had done to my father, the girl must be taken care of. No doubt Liv Thatcher had done right by her, but I saw it as my responsibility. I would have to find a girls' school or a boardinghouse with a woman to teach her the social graces—to grow into the sort of woman this Spanish girl had become.

"Gentlemen?" Raul said with a smile. "I have a large surprise for you. Who wishes to be first?"

I shrugged and followed him back to the walled patio behind the house, taking Gaelyn along by his hand. There in the middle of the courtyard was a huge wooden tub steaming with warm bath water. Raul showed it to us with an inviting gesture.

A bath—my Aunt Matilda! I hadn't had a bath since . . . I couldn't even recall when. Gaelyn indicated I should go first and I stripped and sank into the water. Hot, it was. But it worked into the aching muscles and soaked off the trail dust, the accumulation of travel by land and sea.

When I got out there were fresh clothes laid out for me. And talcum powder, faintly scented. The clothes were nearly right—someone had a good eye for size. I slipped into the black broadcloth pants, the black shirt with silver buttons, and pulled on the new boots which fit better than my old ones—I had grown some since Pa bought them from that drummer out of Helena.

I felt like a new man, and I fancied I cut quite a figure as I examined myself in the mirror. A tall boy, less than twenty but with weathered features that lent me a more mature, sunburned look. My eyes were dark blue set beside that slightly ambitious nose, and my hair, combed back now and wetted down, was reddish brown, curling over my ears somewhat.

I felt like a new man, as they say. And Gaelyn—he *was* a new man!

I barely recognized him. In a new gray suit, wearing a string tie and a white shirt, his hair barbered some, parted in the middle and flattened back, the salt-and-pepper whiskers gone, he cut a fine figure. There was a handsomeness to his features I had never taken notice of. He put out his hand, shaking slightly, but strong still. I recalled the grip he had in them well. More importantly, something seemed to have relaxed in him now that we were free, temporarily.

"I want . . . to thank you proper, Clay." He said hesitantly, but clearly, in a resonant voice. "It took courage to do what you did."

"It took fear, I believe. I had a fear of the shackles and a fear of the Captain."

"Yes," he nodded, "there's always a certain . . . mixture . . . of fear in courage. But you did what was right, and you did it not only for yourself but for another human being. Me."

"Gentlemen!"

Raul came into the room, smiling expansively. "You are back among the living." He walked around us nodding appreciatively, and we were sure to let him know how much we appreciated it.

"But you should thank Pedro," the innkeeper said. "He is the one. Pedro Carnero—there is the man! As you well know, Señor Orduna."

"Yes. There is the man," Gaelyn agreed.

"Come," Raul insisted. "We will have wine, or coffee, what you will. And we will talk. Pedro will be back sometime later, I believe."

We went out onto a low balcony where we watched the sun finish up the day, the lights came on all over Linea del Cielo—and, up on the bluffs above the town, I noticed a campfire.

Gaelyn had a small glass of wine with Raul and they talked some. I mostly listened, learning about the trouble in the area.

"It has gotten a little better," Raul said. "Pedro and Alejandro have organized their small force effectively. General Cedeno's men no longer come to Linea del Cielo. At least they haven't," he said, with his eyebrows raised, looking from me to Gaelyn and back. "Now they may try once more."

"Which way do they come?" I asked him.

"North of town there is a pass. It is the only way. We have men there, however. Plenty of men. It is a strange situation, Clay. The authorities here have become the thieves, the terrorists, preying on travelers and natives alike. The general is a man possessed by the drive toward wealth. And in Mexico City . . . well, it is said he has friends there. We have written letters, even sent men there once. They did not come back."

"That would seem to indicate strong friends indeed. I would not think the *Presidente* would want this man in his army."

"No," Raul agreed. "*El Presidente* does not know of this. Yet he should have been told. There is a man—very high in office. Pablo Carillo. A vice premier responsible for army activities. It is said he may be the man with the deaf ear and the open hand."

"And in the meantime Pedro is the only man between the general and the people."

"*Si*. Without Pedro's army we would be in disastrous straits, Clay. Linea del Cielo was held to tribute in the past. We would pay or our town would be burned. And so we gave out silver, our gold, even— God forgive us—articles from the church. They would have taken them anyway. And Linea del Cielo was not the only town blackmailed with threats of rape and burning, not by far. Here it is as in your own west, law and justice exist only in widely separated pockets. Elsewhere men must make their own law or perish. Here Pedro Carnero is the law."

"And you, Gaelyn? How did you become involved in this?"

"May I answer that?" Pedro Carnero came in from the shadows, trail weary and dusty, his hat in his hand, a rifle slung across his back. He smiled pleasantly, if wearily and sat down opposite me on the railing. Pedro shouted something in Spanish to a man on the street and got a laugh in reply. Then he turned to me, his leathery face scarred on the cheekbones by what looked to be a rope cut, or possibly a quirt or whip. He was a friendly man, with a brilliant smile under his drooping mustache, but a thoroughly cautious one by habit. His rifle never was out of reach, his eyes seemed constantly to be probing the shadows.

"As you see," Pedro said with a heavy shrug, "we are bandits. This is what they call us. If we are killed, there will be no fuss. Maybe some crying by the old women of the villages, but that is all."

"By me, Pedro," a feminine voice said. I turned to see Alma standing in the lighted doorway with Esteban. "Most assuredly by me there would be crying."

"Yes," Raul agreed, "and perhaps by the men as well."

"That may be true. But to strangers, to those in Mexico City, it will be seen as a good thing," the bandit leader said. "This is how it is.

"My friend Gaelyn came to our coast with his brother. They came to bring stolen gold and jewelry to buy opium for California. But Gaelyn did not know that then. He found out, however, and he did not stand for it."

"You confronted your brother?" I asked Gaelyn.

"It did no good," he nodded.

"So Gaelyn and his friend, Polish Joe, took the treasure from the ship and rowed to shore. The soldiers were patrolling and they shot Polish Joe from the cliffs. Then Gaelyn rode on alone. Not knowing where he rode to, but only that his brother and the general must not have the money. We found him wandering in the desert and he came with us to Linea del Cielo."

"But he went back."

"I tried to return to Oregon," Gaelyn said, "to inform the authorities. But the ship I chose to sail on was owned by your uncle too. That was six years ago and the last I saw of land until two days ago."

"The money?"

"It lay buried and I believe is still where I put it. I hurry to get back to Oregon. Now he shall have it. wish that I had given it to Pedro then, but I was in a To buy horses, guns, whatever he needs to throw out this general. Or, perhaps to bribe an ear in Mexico City. I have seen what these . . . 'soldiers' . . . do."

"But the money is not yours either."

"No, Clay. But it is in gold, jewelry, currency. Where did it come from? Many sources and many years past. We cannot return it even if we knew where it came from. So we will leave it where it will help these people."

"And what then?" I asked Gaelyn.

"Then? Then I will stay here with my friends to share their fortunes."

"The firing squad," Pedro said glumly. Then he slapped his knee and stood up. "Give me the wine, Raul. I am not so shy with it as these two. Esteban! Good friend, take a glass. I raise one to you and your happiness, Alma."

We talked for a little while longer and then, still weary, I fell into bed.

Gaelyn had come home. The man I took for an insane, shriveled sailor had proven to be a brave man and a dedicated one. I marked that down in my mind—I would never again judge a man by first appearances. But that night before I fell asleep I determined what I would do. What Gaelyn could not accomplish, I would. The authorities in the United States would be informed of Orduna's dealings. Because I would—I must—return to Oregon. And this time I would be carrying with me the ammunition to sink this devil ship and the others sailing under the flag of Captain Nate Thatcher.

It was no wonder my father had hated these Thatcher brothers, and no wonder they had wanted him dead. I knew my father well enough to know he brooked no dishonesty, no perfidy of this sort. Had he known the truth? Probably. Maybe they had tried to bribe him, or perhaps he had simply taken my mother away from them, disgusted with their dealings. And then he had been murdered.

They would pay for it. I vowed that just as I fell off to sleep, as I was to vow it for many nights to come. How many, I could not have foreseen.

There was one other fleeting thought, or perhaps I had already slipped off into dreaming. I saw the wild mountain meadows in flower, the grass belly high to a horse, the deep blue of spruce along the high ridges, the elk grazing in the aspen-studded valley. And the girl came, a girl not so young, yet full of youth. Graceful as an antelope, long hair flowing behind her as she moved. I was not sure just at that moment if it was Alma or Alicia, but then I knew her. It was Wind on the Waters, and she was calling that she loved me. I turned on my horse and rode away, aware of her tearful calling behind me.

The wind was singing in the trees, and I turned back to tell her that I had changed my mind. "Come along," I said. But then she was gone, and the day had gone cold, the earth barren and icy. I waited awhile, but she did not return, and so I rode on toward the glistening high mountains.

FIFTEEN

We rode out in the cold light of early morning into the valley called Abrazos. Pedro led the way with Alejandro just at his flank on a nearly white horse. Behind them Esteban and Gaelyn rode, Esteban riding a flashy black, his sombrero loose on his back. They had given me a strawberry roan and an old Colt Navy revolver, a Winchester repeater, and a set of Spanish spurs which I hesitated to use on the pony.

We drew up on an oak-covered knoll where the grass was long, golden.

"A mile, no more," Gaelyn said. "Near the river there is a cliff honeycombed with caves."

"You will know which cave it is? Those are the Troneras. Many caves. Thousands, they say," Alejandro said. He was not so tall as Pedro, nor as tall as me for that matter, but thick. A bear of a man with muscles that bulged through his shirt.

"I'll know," Gaelyn assured him. "I counted the caves from the top and from an outcropping to the left at the river bend. Six times four. Yes, I'll know it."

"*Bueno*. Let's ride then before we are seen." Pedro nodded toward some smoke on the high ridge. "Cochimi Indians," he explained. "General Cedeno is generous with them for any information."

The Troneras was a slate-gray cliff rising off the Abrazos River. Nearly three hundred feet high the cliffs were pockmarked with hundreds of caves, perhaps thousands, as Alejandro said. There had been men living in them in ancient times, men who made fine red pottery and ate human meat. Now they were empty, eerie as the wind down the long canyon sang in the cave mouths. I waited with the horses along with Esteban while Gaelyn, Pedro, and Alejandro clambered up the narrow, broken path to the caves.

It was nearly an hour later when Pedro came to the mouth of the cave, whistled shrilly, and waved a jubilant hand.

"We have it!" he called. And then the guns opened up on us.

I saw Pedro jerk and fall back into the cave, clutching his shoulder. Gaelyn's face appeared for a moment behind him and then disappeared again. Up on the bluffs opposite the caves, directly overhead, rifles popped in unison. At least thirty soldiers were up there, and there were others in the river bottom. Upstream I could hear their horses breaking through the cattails and willowbrush.

"They do not see us," Esteban whispered. He was to his horse, swinging into the saddle. "Come on!"

"We can't leave them."

"No. No, *amigo*. We do not leave them. We will go up and behind these on the bluffs. Give them something else to think about."

My heart said no, but my body was already following, stepping into the stirrups of the roan, which bunched its muscles and was off at speed before I had settled.

There was a trail which slanted sharply away from

the soldiers and then circled back to a point behind them, among a bent and broken stand of cypress. We rode hard, the horses lathering under us. All the time we could hear the volleys of rifle fire clattering against the cave faces. Occasionally there was a return shot, and the muted pop of handguns answering the rifles.

Esteban had pulled his horse to a walk and he moved through the woods, his pony tossing its head, a rifle across his saddle. Along the line of the bluffs I saw them. Forty men perhaps, some Indians. Esteban stopped and took his reins in his teeth. As I came even with him he nodded and began firing deliberately.

At the first shot a soldier fell from the bluffs and before anyone could react Esteban had shot another one. This man went down clutching his knee. It was shoot or be killed so I opened up as well. The soldiers were scattering now in panic, their officer standing alone, shouting to them, his saber uplifted. I took him in the shoulder and he began running, grabbing for the pommel of his horse.

We had taken six or seven men, but now the odds were all on their side. The surprise had been our only advantage.

Men rose up from behind the shelter of rocks and deadfall timber, firing, ducking again. On one uniform a splotch of blood appeared. The trees helped some and we moved through them, constantly changing position. They were nearly on top of us now, one group trying to form a rank. Esteban fought crazily. His rifle empty, he fired with two pistols.

His only purpose was to save Pedro and the others. I could see that his own life, at that moment, meant nothing to him. I tapped him on the shoulder and he spun to face me, eyes glazed and wild.

"We've got to run, Esteban."

"Yes," he nodded. He breathed out a long sigh. "All right, let us go."

We wheeled the horses, taking one final shot back over our shoulders. Then we were riding low over our horses' necks, under a hail of gunfire. We dropped into an arroyo and scrambled up the other side. Esteban's pony slipped, hesitated, and went down.

"Esteban!"

The horse had rolled on top of him, crushing him under its kicking weight. I managed to get a hand on him and he swung up behind me. He was bleeding from the chest. My horse, laboring under our weight, finally made the crest and we found our way into a heavily brushed canyon where the world suddenly went silent, with only the rustling wind in the chaparral.

I lay Esteban down in a small clearing, the horse trembling near by. I thought at first his horse had broken some ribs in the tumble, but it proved to be a jagged bullet wound.

"There," Esteban said, waving a limp hand to indicate a scrawny, low shrub, *"Yerba del pasmo.* Boil it, *amigo.* Give me some to drink and wash the wound with the rest."

He could hardly speak, his face twitching with the spasmodic pain. I did as he told me, though the smoke worried me some.

"Good, very good," he grunted as he drank. I held his head up, and when he was through bound up the wound as best I could.

"We'll make it, Esteban," I told him. "We'll make it back."

"Señor, I do not think so."

I turned to face the speaker. There was a man in a torn army uniform directly behind me, and he had a soldier at each shoulder. His pistol was on me and the other two had their rifles ready.

"I think this is the last place you will ever see."

I stood frozen for a moment. This is it, I was thinking. They're going to kill us. But something rose up inside of me. A feeling I had never known before. Out of despair, it grew—a calm, decisive will to battle where there was no other way. A will to fight when fighting was all that was left. It came, this feeling, and it whispered inside of me, reminding me of something I had nearly forgotten.

Dance while she sings . . .

The outsized Colt Navy dangled from my holster and I stood looking into the cold, yellowish eyes of this man who wanted me dead and who would kill the man who lay bleeding beside me. And I drew.

It was quicker than I remembered being. The Colt came up and the first bullet took the leader just above his collar button, driving him backward as his own handgun discharged into the dust. Instantly I dropped to a knee and fired at the man on my left, earing back the hammer on that murderous Colt twice. It was a good thing I had gone down, for one of the guard's rifles cut the air just over my head, near enough to part my hair. But my shots took him in the chest and he sagged to the ground.

The third soldier had not even reacted, it was that fast. Now I had him in my sights as he had me in his. The difference was he was scared and he showed it.

"Drop it. Put it down, hombre, if you will live!"

He hesitated still, then his eyes flickered to his lieutenant and the other soldier and he looked straight into my eyes. He didn't like what he saw there and he nodded slowly, putting down his rifle as if it were a rattler. Then he ran off through the brush and I holstered the Colt.

"Come on, Esteban. He'll bring others back."

"*Amigo*—" Esteban's voice was incredulous. "I never have seen a gun used so quickly. You were a gunfighter in the States, yes?"

"No. Nothing like that. Get on the horse, Esteban, if you can ride."

"*Si*, I will attempt it."

He sat awkwardly in front of me, and with a final glance backward we started off. It hit me then what I had done and I began to shake. I had killed two men in the time it took to blink an eye and could have killed a third.

Dance while she sings . . .

It was an important talent to have, a fearsome ally, this skill which seemed to have come to me naturally. And something to be watched very closely.

I was no gunfighter, but it made me wonder about the man who had taught me. Yule DeLong. What had he really been? And where had he developed such skills as he possessed?

Pedro had gotten away. That was obvious by the frantic searching that was going on along the river bottom. Esteban held out a finger. "That way, Clay. Pedro would go to the Topos. A small river, not far."

We followed the skyline, finally finding the Topos. It was a dry river as many in this country were except when it rains. There were high twin peaks jutting up on either side of the river mouth where it exited a narrow canyon, and I could see why Pedro would have come here. No one could come near without being seen.

We rode up the sandy bottom until Esteban, reeling weakly in the saddle now, showed me a barely discernible path which wound up through the manzanita to a long, narrow bench above the river. The day had grown excessively hot, and the horse labored. There were some thin white clouds high in the blue of the sky, but they did nothing to relieve the fire of the yellow sun.

We found them camped on the bench, under a pair of gnarled oaks.

"Esteban. *Amigo!*" Pedro came to help us, and Gaelyn. Alejandro, I assumed, was keeping watch. Pedro had been hit in the shoulder, and Gaelyn's face was cut up as if he had been showered by rock fragments, but Esteban was by far the most seriously injured.

"Put him here." We laid him gently on the groundsheet and covered him with a blanket. I watched while Pedro worked at Esteban's wounds expertly, closing the ones that had torn open on our ride.

"My herb bag, Gaelyn, if you please."

Gaelyn came back with a sack of canvas filled with sacks of herbs and roots. Pedro selected from these a cactus called *charamatraca*. It grew in slender stalks, climbing vinelike along the rocky ledges, the shafts of the plant marked like snakes. The root of the *charamatraca* is like a sack of clear membrane filled with yellow fluid, and it was this fluid which Pedro chose to make his fresh compresses.

"We are far from any doctor, *amigo*," Pedro said in

response to a remark of mine. "For centuries my people have used every remedy nature offers to us. It must have been the work of thousands of years to discover these medicines beneath rocks, growing high on the bare cliffs, but we needed them or we would have died."

Esteban drank some tea that Pedro boiled from the bark of the sycamore and then slept, comfortably it seemed. After a while Alejandro came into camp, his shirt torn, his face black with what appeared to be gunpowder.

"They do not come, Pedro. But I think we should ride as soon as possible. They may try to take Linea del Ceilo now."

"It will be a time," Pedro said. He nodded toward Esteban whose face was calm, but unusually pale.

"*Bueno*—we will take what comes," Alejandro said stoically. He poured himself a cup of coffee and offered some to me.

"Esteban has told me you are a fighter," Pedro said.

"I had no choice. That will make any man a fighter."

"He has told me you are a wonder with the pistol." He hesitated. "We could use you here, Clay. If you would stay."

The sky was growing dark now, the first stars out, dangling above the endless desert. "You have been good to me, Pedro. And you have a cause which I believe is just."

"Then you will stay?"

"No. I cannot. I have left battles behind me. Battles that must be finished. I wish you luck, and I will see that the authorities in the United States know of this. But I must go in the morning. My journey is a long one."

We climbed out of our rolls in the predawn cool and ate silently. Light was just breaking above the far eastern mountains when I cinched the saddle on the strawberry roan and slid the rifle into my boot.

"I am sorry you are going, *hombre*," Pedro told me.

"I'm sorry too. Perhaps I'll be back one day."

"I hope so. But before you leave, come." He took me by the arm and took me to a clearing just beyond the camp. Gaelyn was there and a shaky Esteban. Between them was a strongbox.

"Take what you want," Gaelyn said, kicking open the lid. "I owe you, Clay. I owe you everything."

"No, you don't, Gaelyn. We're even."

The trunk was filled with jewelry, some gold coins, heavy silver, and a dozen bars of bullion. "I mean it, Clay," Gaelyn Orduna repeated. "I owe you my life, my freedom, my sanity."

"And I owe you as well," Esteban said. "I almost did not live to wed my Alma."

"I mean to travel light," I said. "Besides, I can't get over the feeling that somewhere back along the line this was all stolen by my uncle or men working for him."

"You will need something," Pedro said. He bent over and plucked something from the chest, closing it again after he had done so. "There are times when a man needs a dollar. Take this and God ride with you."

I looked in my hand. He had pressed a ring on me. Ten diamonds flanking a square-cut ruby, it looked very valuable. I tied it around my neck on a leather thong, more to please these men than for any other reason. At least it was light and would provide no encumbrance.

We shook hands all around and by full sunup I was riding north. North toward the far border and toward all that lay beyond it. Oregon, the Thatchers. And a little girl called Wind on the Waters.

SIXTEEN

❖❖❖

I hit the coast in two days and I let my roan have himself a swim in the pounding green surf while I did the same. The gulls whirled and screeched overhead, the long white sands ran forever up and down the Baja peninsula. I lay on the beach drying in the sun, just letting the day travel past. I got to thinking that this stretch of beach was almost the United States too. It would have been but for the blundering clerk who took "The Californias"—meaning Alta or northern California, and Baja or southern California—for a mistake and judiciously changed the treaty to read the singular California, which ceded the territory north of the present line to the States and let Mexico retain ownership of Baja. But it made no difference who owned it—what after all is ownership? What people could actually lay claim to a mountain or a sea, things that would remain after they and all of their kind had returned to dust.

On this superbly pleasant day, the sea softly murmuring against the sand, the sun warm in the crystal sky, the beach was mine to enjoy. What more mattered?

I rode the sands for a while, with my eyes constantly returning to the sea which grew less blue, more green as I traveled north. Once, from the top of a low dune, I saw a slim black hull far out on the ocean. A barkantine, by her rigging—foremast square-rigged, the other two rigged fore-and-aft—it could have been the *Scylla.* I could not tell, but it spurred me on.

On the Tortuga I met a man called Contreras, who offered me beans and beef and a spare horse to help him push some cows to Yuma, and I took him up on it, being low on grub, the roan beat from the wear and tear.

Contreras was a slow-talking man, half-breed, I believe. At the border he told me, "You take them over, Clay."

I shrugged and drove them in, selling them for eighteen dollars a head to a buyer at the fort before I had swung down from the saddle.

The buyer was a squat man with only a fringe of hair and a square jaw where a stubby cigar poked out. "You better watch yourself boy," he advised me.

"Me? What do you mean?"

"You're travelin' with bad company. Wonder why Contreras sent you ahead? He's wanted here. Murdered three men up to Tucson. See that fellow?" He jerked a thumb toward a tall, sleepy-looking man in a faded red shirt. "Lawman from up that way, looking for Contreras. Don't think he didn't notice the brand on these beeves."

"It's nothing to me," I shrugged. I had had no part in whatever had happened in Tucson and after giving Contreras his money I had no intention of ever seeing him again. I was just working as a cowhand for one drive. I told him as much.

"Guess you never heard of guilt by association," the buyer said.

"Heard of it, but I don't believe in it. A man

stands for what he is. By himself. Besides, I had no idea Contreras was wanted."

The cattleman led me to his office where he brought out a bottle of whiskey and began drafting the bill of sale. He shook hands with me and gave me the bank draft and a last warning.

"I'd get back over that border and give this to Contreras. Then I'd ride out before it got light."

"Thanks," I replied, "but I've done nothing to be ashamed of." And as long as I was in town I meant to try some fresh eggs, fruit if I could find any, and buy myself a bath.

As I went out into the street I saw the lawman. Still watching me, he spit out a long stream of tobacco juice into the dusty yellow street. I crossed to the saloon and ordered four eggs and a slab of bacon.

"Mind if I sit down?"

"Go ahead."

The lawman turned a chair around and drew up to watch me eat. I took my time, paying him as little attention as possible. He said nothing while I ate, nor did he remove his hat.

"Go ahead."

"You know who I am? Name's Jack Kesselring. Marshal up to Tucson." He fished in his pocket for a badge which he tossed onto the table. I watched it spin for a moment, dabbed at the corners of my mouth with a napkin, and nodded.

"Pleasure."

"It ain't a pleasure," he hissed. "You're a Contreras man and I want him."

Kesselring was thin, but leather tough, his face slightly off center, his nose a little long. He was tough, and he knew it. I tried to pretend I did not.

"I'm not one of his men. Matter of fact I just was kinda riding along, moving north."

"You'll be going back south," Jack Kesselring said, and he said it hard. He still had his arms crossed over the back of the chair. "And I'm going with you."

"That legal?" I asked innocently. "I thought you were supposed to stay on this side."

"It wasn't legal when he shot Ike and Larry Dovell and my brother, Haight. I'll take him any way I can get him."

"Then that'll be without me. That's the way you'll have to take him."

"Tough one, are you?" He studied me for the first time. Dark, I was, dark as any Indian with my hands toughened by working ropes and lariats, my naturally large frame filled out with the growth of labor. I had caught a scar just under my left eye, shaped like a crescent moon. "You ain't seen tough until you've seen Jack Kesselring on a bad day, boy," he said, leaning close to me, his nicotine breath in my face. "And this is getting to be a real bad day fast."

I slapped a dollar on the table and got up without looking back. Outside the sun was a torch aloft in the yellow sky. Yuma was asleep in the heat of midday, most of the good citizens taking siesta in the shade. The buildings, adobe with a couple of weather-stripped frame hotels. Down near to the Colorado there was a strip of green where palo verde, sage, and some shimmering, silver-leaved cottonwoods competed for the water rights.

I heard them coming before I saw them. I should have tucked into that roan's saddle then and gotten out of Yuma, but I had no real reason to fear the sheriff and his deputies.

"Hey! You there!"

The sheriff was called Bull Planer and he carried a short club with a Smith and Wesson revolver packed high on his belt just behind his hip. The two deputies both carried Henry rifles.

"Yes." I turned to face them square on. I had done nothing wrong, but I stood ready for action, and I let them see that I was ready, letting my gun hand dangle low, my legs slightly bent.

"We don't want your kind in Yuma."

"I'm just leaving."

"You don't understand. We're not quite ready for you to leave either," Bull Planer said. He had a round, puffy face I didn't cotton to and carried about forty pounds too much weight.

"Can't have it both ways, sheriff."

"I can. A fellow law officer from Tucson tells me you're a tough *hombre,* a bad man." The two men beside the sheriff smiled.

"No. Just a citizen trying to move about as he wishes."

He didn't like that answer and was about to step forward. He looked again at the drooping Colt I carried and hesitated. "You up from Mexico?" he asked, almost conversationally.

From the corner of my eye I noticed a blurred movement, a shadow just inside the alleyway. It had to be Kesselring. I wanted to talk my way out of this. But I could feel myself getting angry. They had no right to treat me in this way even if Contreras was all they said he was, and I had my doubts about that too.

"Linea del Cielo," I said. "Just rode up. On my way to San Francisco."

Bull Planer's eyes flashed with curiosity. I still had my attention on the alley. Kesselring would try to follow me from town unless they meant to try something else. In my pocket I had a bank draft worth several hundred dollars. Maybe that was the way the law operated in Yuma.

"Linea del Cielo—ain't that a kinda robbers' roost down there, Rufus?"

"It is," the one called Rufus answered.

"I guess the boy here knows more'n one bandito."

"I was with a man called Pedro Carnero . . ."

"Carnero! He's the bloodiest outlaw ever rode Mexico, excepting maybe Chato Chavez."

"That's not true."

"No? Mexican government has a twenty-thousand-peso reward on that *vaquero*'s head."

"Nevertheless, it's not true."

"Nobody guilty to you, are they, kid?"

I began easing toward my pony. I didn't like the trend this was taking. Then I saw Kesselring come out of the saloon down the street, striding for us. Then who was in the alley!

At that moment Bull Planer would've reached for his pistol. I saw that twitch in his elbow, his jaw go tense, but something stopped him cold.

"Ride, *amigo*!" It was Contreras. He was in the alley with a double twelve leveled on the sheriff and his men. "I will cover you."

I was still watching Kesselring. The marshal had pulled up short and then ducked into an alley. "Kesselring," I told Contreras. "He'll be coming up behind you. Come on!"

I got into the saddle and held my gun on the sheriff while Contreras grabbed his horse out of the alleyway. Then we were riding and the shots rang out as we pounded down the main street of Yuma and across the Colorado River into California, our horses fording the river like they knew the sting of lead, which the roan did.

We stopped on a sandstone ridge, breathing hard.

"They will come," I said.

"No. Bull Planer will not come to California. And I am going back to Mexico, *amigo*. A thousand apologies. I thought there would be no trouble."

"It's all right. My skin hasn't sprung any leaks."

"I am not a murderer, Clay."

"You don't have to tell me."

"Kesselring and his brother and two friends. They came hunting me. I was seeing their sister and they did not like it. There was a fight. I was lucky," he shrugged.

"May your luck hold, *amigo*." I shook his hand and watched as Contreras disappeared over the brushy hills. Then I turned back to what lay before me—the bleak and forbidding desert. And I was a layman here, not knowing where the few unreliable water-holes lay. The only thing I did know as I sat there hot, dirty, tired, was that I could not go back.

SEVENTEEN

———◆———

That first day I did find water. Quite by accident, due only to the roan's keen senses. A small seep running off of the flanks of the Chocolate Mountains, soon returning to the sands which thirstily reclaimed it.

I slept in a narrow canyon, sunburned, exhausted. No matter how tired I was, however, I was determined to travel on within a matter of hours before the devil sun had risen again. Then, as all southern people well knew, I would rest throughout the heat of the day.

On the third day just as we had gained a feeling of confidence the roan caught a hoof in a crevice in a slab of volcanic glass and broke his leg. I said goodbye to the noble animal in a way it never deserved.

I was in that portion of the desert called the Anza-Borrego. I remembered from what Contreras had said that there were several good watering holes, but widely separated. I decided to make for the Palm Canyon spring, which I believed lay generally west.

The countryside was a devil's playground of sand and rocks spewed up in primitive times and left to weather and bake on the rugged hills. Traveling at night had become too treacherous. Gullys opened up before me, jagged escarpments, and everywhere there were rocks to stumble over and fall.

But the day was a nightmare of heat and light. Palm Canyon—I knew the Butterfield Stage ran through there or near to it. That was my only chance. I could no more walk to the coast than I could fly.

I stumbled into the station three days later, branded by the sun, my feet torn to shreds. It was night and I called before I went in. There had been sporadic Indian trouble though I had seen neither man nor beast excepting a magnificent desert bighorn sheep too far off to shoot, and so solitary and beautiful that I would not even have considered it if I hadn't been half starved.

The lights went on in the station in answer to my calls and I hobbled down, the station dancing crazily in my vision.

"Lord! It's a white man," the man said. He helped me inside and with a quick look out locked the door again.

"Where did you ever come from?"

"Yuma."

"Yuma . . . why that's not possible. Emma, get the man some water. A little water."

"Beats me how he found us," the woman said.

"I was told where Palm Canyon is," I said, drinking thirstily.

"Palm Canyon. You must've missed that two days back, mister. This is the San Felipe station and we ain't been open more'n three days since we had to scoot on out of here. Indian raid. Blind luck is what you got. You've no right to be alive."

From what I learned later he was right. I had no right to be alive, but it felt almighty good. These folks were the McConklins and they took care of me for four days until the next stage came through, traveling empty but for a miner heading back to the mountains.

We were in the shadows of the mountains now. The Lagunas, they called them, and the stage took a long winding grade called Banner up and over to the gold town of Julian. It was hooting pretty good, a few shots rang down the main street. I slept in the coach, just grateful for the coolness we had overtaken as we crested the peaks. We were up nearly six thousand feet, but the night wasn't particularly cool. Not to me.

I awoke refreshed the next morning as we switched drivers and rolled on out toward Santa Ysabel. From there we made it in a day and a half to the coast.

It was a cool blue day in San Diego, the sky cloudless but for a gray fog farther out to sea. I walked along the docks until I found a vessel bound for San Francisco.

"Had any experience, or you lookin' for a free ride?" the skipper asked, peering at my cowboy outfit, my beat-up boots and guns.

"I've sailed some," I said grimly.

It was twelve days up the coast, putting in once at Santa Barbara for water. It was in San Francisco that I first saw a wanted poster with my name on it.

Wandering down Front Street, I stopped near a police station to ask my way. There it was, hanging on the wall behind the dark-eyed cop. I read it while he talked.

"Assaulting an officer of the law, rustling, and robbery," it said. I eased on out of the station nice and slow.

I don't know where they dug up that robbery business, but in Yuma I figured Bull Planer and Kesselring could probably sure enough make the other charges stick. I was suddenly wishing I was back in the desert.

It was growing dark along the docks. I walked on, liking the damp air, the sounds of fish mongers. But I had me some worrying to do. Kesselring wanted me. In a way that was good—it meant Contreras had gotten out of the country. But Kesselring figured I knew where he was, especially after I'd admitted to staying in Mexico for a time.

"You in a bind, ain't you?"

I turned to face the man. It was Tull Gibbs, a mate on the ship. I didn't like the man particularly, he had an arrogant way about him, but we had managed to stay out of each other's way.

"In trouble?" How could he know. Kesselring might be fast working, but not that fast.

"Just thought I'd let you know. Gang of boys come huntin' you tonight. Skipper tried to keep 'em off, but they bulled right on."

"Orduna!" I said it out loud.

"That's right. I never met him myself, and I don't want to, but the skipper has and he said I should shake a leg to let you know they're layin' for you."

"Thanks, Gibbs. I know we weren't friends."

"We were shipmates," he shrugged. I watched him amble off down the winding cobblestone road.

Of course Orduna would have men watching for me, knowing I would try to make my way back. And for Orduna I meant trouble. I had already destroyed his opium shipment, freed his brother, and now I would go to the authorities. On top of that Nate Thatcher would be furious with his sea captain for allowing me to escape. Orduna would find me if he could. And he would have to kill me.

Now, with the trouble in Yuma I would have to

face arrest myself in order to report what I knew. That was a risk I would have to take, however; there was no way I could ever face myself again unless I did what had to be done.

"Clay?"

I spun around, my hand dropping to my Colt. In the near darkness it was awhile before I made out the familiar face.

EIGHTEEN

"McCafferty!" I couldn't believe my eyes, but he was standing there, fit, plump as ever.

"You shouldn't be on the streets. Orduna's looking for you. He knows you're in Frisco," Mac said, taking my shirt sleeve.

"I know it. And I've got to avoid his thugs at least until morning. When the Federal offices open, I'm going to have a talk with the Merchant Commission."

"He'll kill you!"

"He'll kill me anyway if I give him the chance," I shrugged. "I've got to do it."

"Come on, I know a place," McCafferty said. We wound through the narrow alleys until we came to a tiny coffee shop without a sign. We sat down in the dimly lighted place and Mac ordered coffee for us.

"But you," I said, "you're looking well. Didn't Orduna . . . ?"

"Aye, he punished me. He beat me astern and amidship. Yet I've been on his ship a long while. And it wasn't me disturbed the opium."

"And you told him where Gaelyn was going," I suggested softly.

"Yes. Shamed I am," he said lighting his pipe. "I remembered what he said about Linea del Cielo. But I think they knew anyway, Clay."

I let it pass. That was gone by. The coffee was good, with just a touch of chicory and a sweetness that was not from sugar.

"You'll be going to the authorities?"

"Yes."

"And then to Oregon?"

"If I can . . . they may arrest me . . ." The room was smoky, hot. The proprietor leered at me over the counter, a waxed mustache hanging from his lip like a coiled, black snake.

"Arrest you, you say?"

McCafferty was leaning back, his arms crossed over his chest. His pipe drooped from his mouth and he nodded frequently, his cherubic cheeks red beside his white whiskers.

"Damn you, McCafferty . . ."

The room had begun to sway violently, and the heat and smoke became unbearable. The coffee cup . . . I threw it on the floor and through a blurred, distorted lens I saw three or four thugs coming at me, Coombs among them. At the door stood Orduna, his black eyes staring, his mouth cracked in a soundless bellow of laughter. I stood and tried to swing out, but my arms were leaden.

"You!" I stretched a hand out toward McCafferty, but he seemed to drift off, becoming disembodied, his face melting like a candle. Then the drug did its work and I went out.

The voices were muffled. The room gray, dark, and damp. It was a room and not the hold of a ship at least. The corners met square and the rolling was in me, not in the deck.

"Our young friend's awake at last."

"So he is. A shame . . . better he'd stayed under."

"No. I wanted him to feel it."

I got slowly to my knees. My elbows and knees were torn, from being thrown into the room I supposed.

They stood in a circle around me, backlighted by a candle. Like vultures or jackals. Orduna was there, Coombs. The man from Port Keyes—Scully. And pressed back against the wall, McCafferty.

"Boots McCafferty, you've done me wrong. Twice a Judas," I panted. I struggled to my feet, pressing flat hands against the wall, but just as I had gotten erect a foot lurched out and knocked my legs out from under me.

"You have offended me, young man," Orduna said. He was hovering over me, his scarred face demonic in the faint light. Coombs was grinning stupidly and I wished I had a minute to get my hands on his throat. "You have offended me and cost me a great deal of money. And my brother is gone. You owe me a great deal." Without warning his foot shot out and caught me over the kidney and I sagged to the floor, coiling up to protect myself. Coombs had a sap, Scully a lead pipe.

"I will collect it," Orduna said.

"You'll try. But you'd better kill me because I'll tear your head off if I get the chance."

At that a boot toe landed again and I heard a rib crack. "I'll not kill you. Your good uncle wishes to speak to you. But," he snarled, "I'll have you so that you'll carry out none of your threats. You'll be a cripple, boy. Pure a cripple."

I saw McCafferty, a sickly expression on his face edging toward the door. He couldn't meet my eyes. Panting, I got to my knees, holding my side which was shot through with pain. All right, they would beat me, but I would have my shots.

"Please, Captain, I won't ever . . ." Then I drove myself at him, my fists driving into his face. I saw his cheek split, the blood spew out. Coombs came toward me, swinging his sap, but I caught his wrist and nearly broke his arm. He yelled with pain and I kicked him viciously on the kneecap, shattering it.

I saw a shadow and turned just out of line as Scully hammered at my skull with his pipe. It caught my shoulder, the pain shooting through my arm. Enraged, I managed to get my hands on his throat, tearing at it until his eyes hung out, his tongue choking him as he turned blue.

Then something went off in my head like a cannon shot. I turned to face it, but I was staggered. Coombs had hit me with his blackjack and Orduna had his pistol out. He clubbed me with it, and I felt the hot blood running down from my scalp. I clutched at Orduna's face and then his coat, but I found no grip. He clubbed me again with the pistol butt and I went down.

"Finish him," Orduna screamed, the blood from his face staining his navy blue coat.

"Thatcher won't like it," Coombs said.

"Finish him. The hell with Thatcher."

Coombs shrugged and turned to me, lifting his blackjack. I watched him coolly prepare to kill me, saw the indifference in his eyes. Then the door burst open and McCafferty was there pointing the way for a gang of blue uniformed policemen.

The cops rounded up the thugs while McCafferty came to me. "I'm sorry," he kept saying. "I'm damn sorry. It's the morphine—where else can I get it? I needed it, Clay."

The police sergeant hustled the three sailors out of the room, then he looked closely at me.

"You're beat up some. How d'ya feel."

"Not bad."

"Good." He was a big Irishman, clean shaven, hard. "Now I'll be taking you along as well. Or aren't you Clay Rourke?" He unfolded the piece of paper he had with him and smoothed it out on his knee. A wanted poster, the same one I had seen that morning.

"I don't know why I just don't let you crooks kill each other off," he grunted. Then he pulled me roughly to my feet and dragged me from the room. McCafferty stood there bewildered, watching as the door closed behind us.

There was a wagon in front of the dockside building with bars for walls and two bench seats. Coombs, clutching his knee, was sitting in it already and Orduna was being shoved up roughly by two burly policemen. These San Francisco cops were used to the tough ones. The Barbary Coast with its thugs and smugglers, shanghaiers and bloody intergang fighting, the notorious Sydney Ducks, privateers and swindlers were everyday challenges. They were a no-nonsense crew, and with good reason, tough men.

A horse walked slowly along the wharf as Orduna was put into the wagon, its hoofs clacking on the planks. The lights from the city danced on the waters of the bay. From there I could see the sweep of the San Francisco Bay, and up onto Nob Hill where the wealthy and famous lived as well as down toward the Embarcadero where two dozen full time gangs spent their time in the not-so-fine art of shanghaiing, and across the bay to the Chinatown where the acrid smell of opium filled the alleyways.

Scully was thrown in as the police sergeant held me by the collar.

"All right, young man," he said, tugging me toward

the wagon. At that moment I went slack, shrugging off my coat. I ducked under his arm and in another second I was into the cold water, swimming back under the wharf. I could hear their voices and the clack of their boots above me.

I clung to a barnacle-covered piling while the currents toyed with me.

It was Orduna I heard screaming. "You've got to go after him."

"I'm not ordering anyone in the water."

"He's a killer. Shoot him!"

"Through the wharf? We'd have a better chance of shooting a fish. Roll them out, Harry," the sergeant said. The cop moved off with the jail wagon, Orduna cursing.

I knew they would be waiting up there, searching the shore nearby. But the docks were a maze of wharfs and anchored ships, and I was as good as free.

I dragged myself onto dry land a quarter of a mile to the south. At that point there was a dark cove, with no building or light in sight. Still I got quickly off the beach and started moving north. Toward Oregon.

Fatigued as I was I plodded along, and it was only by good luck and not by alertness that I saw the lone rider moving along the road. I drew off into the bushes and waited while he passed. He was smoking a pipe, riding a slow walking bay gelding. By the cherry glow of his pipe I caught a glimpse of his features. It was Marshal Kesselring!

I was sure at first, but as he passed and the darkness closed around me again I was not so certain. How far would a man go, even a slightly demented one as I believed Kesselring to be, to track down the killer of his brother? Following me to San Francisco seemed absurd. How could he have known where to look?

I knew that it was possible, of course. With a little luck he would have discovered that I caught the Butterfield stage for San Diego, and he might have asked around on the docks there, with someone remembering me, the ship I had sailed on, and where she was bound.

He had wanted me badly enough to put out that wanted poster.

Suddenly I was tired. Unbearably so. My head throbbed from being clubbed, my feet hurt, I was wet and cold and worn out mentally. The farther I traveled toward my goal the more snarled things became. I had developed strong and plentiful enemies since leaving Montana. Perhaps I had been wrong in taking up the vengeance trail, in seeking my father's killer. Yet I could not have let it pass.

Wearily, I stumbled on until I found a hollow deep in a thicket. I crawled into it until I was concealed completely, and curled up in a ball I slept, my night filled with confused, terrifying dreams.

NINETEEN

In the colorful light of dawn, Port Keyes was a picture-book seaport. On the gently curved Oregon coast, the mountains rising up behind, deep green, tending to a rich gray, the town still slept in the early hours although several small fishing vessels were already out on the green waters of the Pacific. The houses, mostly white with red roofs, were nicely spaced along winding roads, and the grass was rich on the knolls to the north and the east, spotted here and there with carpets of white-and-golden wildflowers. But for me Port Keyes was an Armageddon, and here my battles would be fought. There would be blood in the streets before I had seen her for the last time, this I knew.

Main Street was deserted as I walked into it, save for a few industrious shopkeepers sweeping off the boardwalk and the restaurant which was already finished with breakfast for the fishermen. A baby was crying somewhere uptown and I heard the creaks and groans of tackle from the stable. The saloon was locked up tight.

"Open up!" I pounded on the door for what seemed to be an hour. An older couple passing by glanced at me dubiously and hurried on. The door opened with a jerk and Earl stood there in his pants and undershirt.

"What the hell do . . . ? Clay?" He examined me like a curious insect. "Clay Rourke. Lord, boy! We thought you were dead. You left and never came back. We figured the Thatcher brothers had strapped you to an anchor and thrown you over the side."

"They pretty nearly did." Sketchily, I told him the story. "Then I got a ride with a mule skinner up to Portland. From there I walked. But Earl, I've got to see Wind on the Waters. How is she?"

"Come on in, Clay. Man, you've gotten hard, haven't you?" He nodded with apparent satisfaction.

"The girl."

"Yes," he sighed, "the girl. Will you have some coffee with me?"

"I want to see her, Earl."

He stopped, the pot still in his hand, his burly back to me. "She's gone, Clay."

"Gone! But why would she go? She couldn't have gone, she had nowhere."

"Sit down." Earl gave me a cup of coffee despite my protests and nodded to a table. I took down a chair and waited to hear what he had to say.

"Liv wouldn't have let her go," I said, trying to grasp it. Wind on the Waters was gone.

"Liv Thatcher is dead, Clay."

"Dead?" That took even longer to soak in.

"I'll tell you what happened. You set and rest for a minute. Drink the coffee. You appear to need it."

I did need it, and it warmed me, but I needed to know more. Earl shrugged slightly, his big forearms flat on the table. He looked at me, his dark eyes houndlike. "They drove her crazy," he said.

"Who did, Earl?"

He motioned me to be silent, so I let him tell it in his own way.

"They found out that she had taken you in, told you some things, encouraged you. Them Thatchers were always a vengeful bunch, and they never took to Liv, being contrary as she was.

"They began to have men hanging around the porch out front. Anybody wanted to come through the doors would have to pass through them and risk a licking. There was some bad fights just outside, but only the tough ones wanted a drink bad enough to trade punches with Jay Thatcher and those rowdies of his. After a time nobody came.

"Then things started to pick up a little. Six barrels of whiskey I found one morning. Bashed in with sledges. All of the windows were busted out, and one night they tried to set fire to the place.

"Liv, she run out in her wrapper, the fire crackling all around her. We pitched water on it from the rain barrels and we got her out. But Liv, she was never the same after that. Finally, about four, five months back she passed on in her sleep."

"And Wind on the Waters?"

"Yes. Wind on the Waters." Earl sighed heavily and got up, filling his cup again. "You see how that was, don't you?" he asked, returning. "A young girl living in a saloon with nobody to watch her. Soon the ladies of the town got to clucking about it. Mrs. Miles Thatcher chief among 'em, along with Mrs. Rezak— that's the mayor's wife. So they decided to send her off to school."

"Where is this school?"

"I'll tell you." My impatience was disconcerting to Earl. I could tell that retelling it had brought him some pain, so I waited, restraining myself.

"There was a lady lived here—Irma Grossman. An old widow lady with no family anyone knew of. Seems, however, she has some family ties with upper crust folks in Europe. Bavaria, I believe, or Prussia. Anyway, her cousin was staying with her. Fine woman named Schumann. She seen Wind on the Waters while this was going on and took a shine to her. The girl had a fine, proud way to her, Clay. She kept a-sayin' she was going to stay right here until you came back. But even I could see it wasn't right. Not in no saloon.

"Upshot of it, short and sweet, is that this lady Anna Schumann took Wind on the Waters with her when she went back home."

"Where was that? Home?"

"Denver, Colorado. Funny thing was Wind on the Waters was agin' it all the way, but she found out they were going to Denver and she did a turn about. Said she had an idea you might be going there."

"I will be now, that's for sure. But first I've got some other business."

"Stay out of the Thatcher's pasture, Clay," Earl warned me. "You've seen no men like these, no matter where you've been, and I take it you've seen some."

"I'll need a handgun and a rifle."

"I mean it, Clay. They'll cut you up."

"I mean it too, Earl! Lord, how I mean it."

It was full light when I went out, the shadows long on the dusty street. From the center of town I could see the yellow house on the hill. The house where the Thatcher brothers lived and plotted their crimes. I started up there, the spanking new Colt .44 on my hip, the Winchester in my hand. I saw someone run off toward the sheriff's office and a few people shuttering up their homes.

I rapped hard on the door and a maid answered it.

"Nate Thatcher here? Captain Nate Thatcher?"

The maid, a slight, older woman stepped back, her hand to her throat. She was frightened, and she had a right to be. Standing there in my travel-worn clothes, rifle to hand, unshaven, and dirty I could guess what I looked like.

"Yes, sir. He's having his breakfast with Mister Miles Thatcher. But they can't be disturbed, sir."

"It's all right," I said, pushing her gently aside. "I'm their long-lost nephew."

I walked straight through the house, my boots noiseless on the blood-red carpet. I never paused; from some childhood memory I knew just where the dining room was and I opened the door to find my two uncles at their breakfast at a sumptuously set table.

"Good morning."

"Who in the hell . . . ? You must be Clayborne Rourke."

"I am Clay Rourke."

The older of the two men was Miles Thatcher, the merchant who dealt in furs . . . and opium. He wore a full set of muttonchop whiskers and was slightly bald. The darker, younger man was Captain Nate Thatcher. His face was that of a pirate, lean, scarred, and sharp. He threw down his napkin and stood.

"Sit down, uncle," I said mildly. The muzzle of my rifle came up slightly and he sat down respectfully.

"It's a pleasure to see you," Miles said, sipping his coffee from a tiny china cup. "It's been years, since you were a babe."

I didn't like his easy way and I glanced around me at the china cabinet, the french windows curtained in green silk, and the white door to the kitchen beyond.

"Join us," Miles Thatcher said, his hand gesturing to an empty chair.

"Thank you, no. Your breakfast is over, too. In fact, an end to a lot of things is at hand."

"The boy is mad—he has it from his father," Miles said smugly.

"Get out of here with you!" Captain Nate Thatcher was not one for civilities.

"I mean to. And you with me. You see, not only did Orduna let me escape, he let me find out what this great trade empire of yours is based on, Uncle. And I will see that it ends. I've already told my story in San Francisco," I said, bluffing.

"Utterly mad."

"Get out of Port Keyes," Captain Nate said, "before I have you killed."

"As you had my father killed! You and you! As you killed Liv Thatcher, your own sister, with your spiteful hatred. As you have killed and tormented countless others with the poison morphine you supply them with! You'll not kill me, animal!"

Suddenly Nate Thatcher snapped to his feet, throwing the table toward me, but I stepped back and then lunged forward, clubbing him across the bridge of the nose with my rifle butt. He sagged to the floor, blood spewing from his broken nose. Miles Thatcher still sat there, cup in hand, although the table was spilled all over the floor.

"Get your hat," I told him. It was hanging on a rack nearby. He nodded condescendingly and did so, tugging his vest down to straighten it. I picked up

Nate by his collar and shoved him in front of me toward the door.

We walked through into the living room, with a door closing hurriedly as a servant ducked for cover. The front door stood open and I marched them onto the porch.

There were four of them there, sitting their horses.

The man in the front I recognized instantly as Jay Thatcher, the notorious bully. He was fleshy from much drink and his hands were broken and scarred. There were pouches under his eyes and his massive shoulders strained at the seams of his coat. Beside him was the big man who, along with Scully, had shanghaied me. The others I hadn't seen. They all had weapons out and trained on me with the exception of Jay Thatcher, who sat his horse haughtily, a nasty glare in his eyes.

"Suppose you put down that gun," he said in a gravelly voice, "before we have to hang and butcher you, boy."

"Get back," I told him. "Because I've no intention of doing that. And if you choose to shoot, remember the Thatchers are going first."

I nudged Miles with the muzzle of my Winchester.

"You," I said in a low voice. "You'll be the first. Then the captain here."

"Jay . . ." Miles's voice was trembling, he knew there was no bluff in me then. These were the men who had done me harm.

"He won't shoot," Jay said, but he looked at me, the mark of my troubles cut into my face, and he knew even as he said it that it was a lie. And he knew I would take some of them with me even if they shot me to pieces.

"Get out of the way! Now," I told them before he had time to think on it, "ride on out!"

Reluctantly, they turned their horses and began to walk them slowly back toward town. "All right then," I said, poking Nate Thatcher, "let's go on down too."

"They'll hang you! And if they don't, we'll have you skinned alive. And we know the men to do it."

These were men used to having their own way, and always before, bullying and threats had gotten it for them. But I had waited too long for this and I could not be bribed nor frightened any longer.

The streets were filled with men. Milling around they grumbled and called, children ran shouting toward the center of town as I marched the Thatcher brothers forward. Finally, in front of the sheriff's office we stopped and stepped onto the boardwalk.

A crowd of fifty men or so had gathered and they pushed forward. I saw the sheriff moving hurriedly through the crowd—he was a lanky man with a patch over his left eye and his pistol drawn.

"Suppose you tell me what's going on," he said as he reached us. He was sputtering with anger.

"I'm Clay Rourke," I announced, speaking so that everyone could hear me. "These are my uncles, along with that fat man over there," I said nodding toward Jay Thatcher who came off his saddle with that remark. Then I proceeded to tell them a part of my story.

"It's a damn lie! Take him out and hang him," Jay Thatcher interrupted. He shoved a couple of his bullies forward and at that movement the entire crowd surged at me.

"Stop! Get back, Carry, Bingham!"

It was Earl, still in shirt sleeves. He stepped up beside me on the boardwalk, a shotgun in his hands.

"Get down, barkeep. You got no business in this."

"I got business in it," Earl shouted back. "Liv Thatcher was my boss and a lot more. You listen to the kid here. Hear him out. Sheriff Bonds?"

"That's the least we can do," the sheriff nodded, spitting out a chaw of tobacco. "Go light, Earl," he warned him. "You get to waving that scattergun around you're liable to hurt someone."

"Go ahead, Clay," Earl said to me, his eyes on the citizens of Port Keyes, most of whom were for the Thatchers simply because they knew them; they were a part of the community and I was a down at the heels drifter.

"This man, Miles Thatcher, respected citizen, is a smuggler of opium. His brother Nate sails for the opium fleet and so does Orduna. I've been on the *Scylla*, and saw the cargo she held."

"That's absurd," Miles flashed.

"It's true. As true as the fact you had my father killed. He knew as much as I do, I suppose."

"We didn't have him killed. What for? He was gone away for a long while, far away."

"Wait . . ." Earl interrupted us. "There's a ship coming in this morning. The *Glen Maire*. That's a Thatcher ship."

"So what?"

"Why not send a citizens' committee to meet the *Glen Maire*? Sheriff? Mayor Rezak? Let's see what it is she's carrying."

"No! You have no right at all," Miles said. "Phil? For heaven's sake!"

Mayor Rezak had come slowly forward and he shook his head. "I don't believe it, Miles. But the citizenry has a right to know."

"I won't allow it."

"Miles, be reasonable," Mayor Rezak said. A concerned look had clouded his eyes. He tried to penetrate Miles Thatcher's thoughts.

"Mayor?"

"I think we'd better, sheriff."

"This is ridiculous. It's illegal!"

"I think not. The judge will give us a warrant. Miles—I pray it isn't true; but if it is, I've no truck with traffickers."

We went down to the docks, the whole town it seemed and the *Glen Maire* came in shortly after two o'clock, sails cut, drifting to anchor. The mayor, the sheriff, and six or seven prominent citizens rowed out in a longboat while we stood by.

"You know, Clay," Earl said, "there's a chance the *Glen Maire* has no contraband at all. There's a-plenty of furs brought in by Thatcher ships."

"There's a chance," I agreed.

"If there's nothing there . . . they'll kill you sure, boy."

We waited. The shore party clambered up the ladder and disappeared into the ship. We stood silently on the beach, all eyes on the low hull of the *Glen Maire*. It was a sunny, cool day. A few high clouds drifted in front of the sun, casting shadows on the long cove.

"They must be tearing it apart," someone remarked.

There was no answer. A few men had gone off, but most remained, sitting on the beach or standing with arms crossed.

"Here they come!" a man with field glasses yelled.

The boat came slowly in, the mayor in the prow. The oars dipped into the dark surface of the water.

The longboat came slowly to shore, at the last catching a thrust of light surf.

The mayor was expressionless, the sheriff tight-lipped. They walked up to us slowly in the sand. "Put that gun down, Earl!" the sheriff said sharply.

Miles Thatcher's face broke with relief. He half turned toward me.

"Rourke," the sheriff snapped. "Hand over that rifle!"

"Then you found nothing?"

He took the rifle from me and eased the hammer forward. "We found it all right," he said. "Captain's quarters under the bunk in a sextant case. Opium."

"Miles Thatcher. Nate Thatcher. You're under arrest for smuggling."

The mayor walked straight past us, wagging his head. The crowd followed after them, some on ponies racing ahead with the news. Then the beach was empty. Earl slapped my shoulder and walked off. I waited. The ship rested low in the water, the clouds had begun to fill the gaps where blue sky showed. It was likely to rain. A family of sandpipers raced along the beach on stilt legs, looking for sand crabs.

I turned and walked slowly toward Port Keyes.

Something played softly in my mind. Miles Thatcher had said they had not killed my father. He had gone from Port Keyes, far away to Montana, and years ago. Why, he had asked, would they have killed him? He had said they—these Thatcher brothers—did not kill him. Thing was, I half-believed him.

TWENTY

——◆◆——

I found Earl sitting alone in the locked-up saloon. He was in the room that had been Liv Thatcher's, sitting on the bed, her picture in his hands. He looked up as I went in, and there were tears in his dark eyes.

"Maybe I should have asked her. Maybe she would have married me, Clay. Just maybe." He shook his head. "Who am I kidding? She was a lady. A classy lady. I started to ask her . . . a hundred times."

He got up slowly and put the picture in the bureau.

"Anybody asking for me?"

"No, Clay. They won't need you. Sheriff and the mayor found the opium. Any testimony you could give would just be second hand. They'll lock 'em up and throw the key out, I expect."

"What about Jay?"

Earl shook his head. "They can't touch him. Miles and Nate were in this up to their ears, but they can't pin a thing on Jay."

"Then he'll be wanting my hide."

"He will. You'd best light out."

"No. I'll give him his wish."

"He's a brute, Clay. He's gouged and bitten, knifed and clubbed more men than you've known. He's rough and tumble, but canny in his fighting too. He's had a lot of practice,'' he added grimly.

"He won't get off scot-free," I promised Earl, "not if I can help it."

"There's some things that belonged to your mother," Earl said, waving a hand toward the bureau. "Not much—there never is."

"I'll take them," I said. There was a portrait of my mother as a very young woman. Beautiful, she was, her head tilted proudly, a devilish gleam in her eye, an intelligent high brow. I saw a bit of myself there, and a lot of Liv. There was a lace scarf, yellowed with the years, and a plain gold band which I slipped on my little finger. There was also a tintype of my father, when he still wore mustaches, with some members of his Civil War company. One face jumped out at me from that group. Next to my father was the man named Jake!

"Have you ever seen this man, Earl?"

Earl examined it and shrugged. "No, can't say I have. Who is he?"

"Jake Wadell. He was with the men who killed my father and tried to kill me. I shot him—and bandaged him up afterward. I saw him in Port Keyes . . . at least I thought I did. Didn't you ever see him before? He must have been working for the Thatchers!"

"No, Clay. I've never seen this fellow. And if he worked for the Thatchers, I sure would have."

"Then why . . . ?" Why had he followed me to Port Keyes?

There was a pounding at the front door, then the sounds of wood splintering and angry, drunken cursing. I knew who it was.

"Get out, Clay! No one could fault you for it."

"I'd fault myself." I wrapped my mother's things

up carefully and straightened myself up, removing my gun belt. Jay Thatcher was standing before me, filling the doorway with his bulk.

"I've come for you, boy. I've come to have my due."

Never had I seen such unbridled hatred, nor such confidence. He had it in his mind that he was going to crush my bones, break me as easily as he might tear loose a roasted chicken's wing. Maybe he would. But I wanted him. I wanted him badly, wanted to break this man in the only way that would hurt a bully like Jay Thatcher—with my two hands against his.

He wasted no time and started forward across the saloon floor, his meaty fists uplifted. But I hadn't been raised shy, and I put down my head and drove into him, taking the wind from him as I drove him back and out into the brilliant daylight of the street.

"Someone call an undertaker," Jay called over his shoulder. Then he stepped in, winging heavy punches at my head. I ducked a left, just slipped another, and then took a right hard on the cheek. I staggered aside and fell into another left, glancing off the top of my skull.

I was aware of a crowd gathering around us, the dust of the street, the blood running in a thin trickle down from my cheekbone, but the battle had begun and my senses were focused on only one man.

I shook off the numbness in my head and crouched low, coming in. Jay hadn't expected an attack and I caught him off balance, chopping short, telling blows to his wind and the kidneys.

"So," he puffed, falling back, "you are game after all. I wouldn't have expected it from a son of Jeb Rourke."

"My father whipped you," I said, spitting out blood to do so, "and I mean to nail up that bloated carcass of yours to the stable wall as well."

Thatcher was stung by the remark. He didn't think I could know about that terrible fight, but I recalled it, young as I had been. A few folks in the crowd did too, and I heard some of them cheering me on.

Jay Thatcher literally hurled himself through the air, his full weight catching me and taking me to the earth, the breath out of me. Desperately I pushed out with the heel of my hand under the point of his chin, bringing up a knee at the same time. He was clawing at my eyes with thumbnails especially sharpened just for such business. Frantic for my vision I kneed him again, this time catching him where he lived. I twisted out from under him, but astoundingly the big man was already to his feet, and there was blood in his eyes.

Jay Thatcher went all of two hundred and sixty pounds, a good share of it hard muscle under a deceptive layer of fat, and when he landed his punches, it rocked me to my heels. I began circling to his right, staying away from a hooking left hand which had been doing the most damage. Still he got me steadily, my lighter jabbing punches bouncing off his jaw like it was a cast iron pot belly stove and not a man's face at all.

"You got to get inside, Clay!" Earl shouted and I nodded. First I feinted a light left which caused Jay to duck and bob away, then I brought my right across catching him flush, stinging him. His guard went up against another punch and I came in, working hard on his midsection.

I let go with a furious right, with all the mustard I had in the jar behind it, and as it sunk into his soft belly, I heard and felt a rib go. Jay winced with pain, but pain was nothing new to this brawler; it was how he made his living.

He began bulling me forward, shoving me with both forearms, smashing them into my chest, throat, and chin. Frantically I chopped back with short, ineffective punches. I was sweating through my torn shirt, bleeding from several cuts, one of them over my left eye was a serious one. But I still had my strength, and Jay Thatcher, I could tell now, was tiring. Those granite hard fists were not falling with the same crushing effectiveness as they had. If I could only last . . .

My heel caught the edge of the boardwalk as I was shoved back and I went down hard, my head cracking against the planks. Jay aimed a kick at me, but I rolled aside. Again he tried a kick, this one meant to break my skull, but I caught his heel coming by and forced it upward as it glanced off me. Jay went down like a felled tree.

I tried to leap for him, but could barely stagger to where he lay. He came to his knees and swung wildly with twin uppercuts. I put a straight right into his nose and saw the flesh split there, his blood spattering us both.

He came slowly to his feet and I came in again. I had only one thought—keep him down. Keep the big man down. My foot hooked behind his ankle and I jerked hard, throwing the best right I could manage at the same time. He parried with his hands but went down from the tripping.

"Boy . . ." he wanted to say something, but whatever it was would not come for lack of breath. He was on his knees again and I went in again, my arms heavy as lead weights, my legs rubbery, my chest filled with fire. I brought up a knee and caught him under the chin and he fell back, his tongue split, his mouth filled with blood.

Savagely, he growled and tried to rise. He was on all fours, pawing at the earth, going for my legs, but I would not let him have them. I stood away, fists dangling limp at my sides, the sun glazing my eyes.

He arched his back and rose, turned from me. As he came around with a wild roundhouse I caught him square.

I had Jay Thatcher now, and I knew it. His blows were wild, ineffectual. Each time I caught him now I caught him crisply; he was no longer able to bob his head in time to parry.

I stuck him with a sharp right to the temple and another to the heart, this one with the full force of my rolling shoulders behind it and he stopped dead, eyes blank, his face a puttylike mass of red and purple. Again he waved at me weakly, but the fire, already gone from his blows, was now gone even from his eyes and it was only a fighter's instincts that kept him going.

I winged in a hard left hook and another, and Jay Thatcher began staggering, wandering in a circle, swinging at those in the crowd, not knowing who or where he was. At the ends of his arms two open palms waved. He hadn't the strength to make a fist.

"I'll kill you!" he muttered, his speech as slurred as a drunk's. "I'll kill you all. I'll kill you!"

One by one the crowd began to wander off. I stood bracing myself, my legs wide apart. Jay Thatcher still walked in his aimless circle, slapping at shadows, cursing me, himself, his brother, and all of Port Keyes.

"Come on, Clay." Earl threw an arm over my shoulder and I almost collapsed. He took me back into the saloon, the blathering of Jay Thatcher still sounding in the street.

It was cool and dark in the saloon, and I sat across the table, my hands to my head. After a while Earl returned with a pan of hot water.

"Soak your hands in this. It'll cut the swelling some."

As I did he worked on my cuts, applying a plaster to my eyebrow and cheekbone. The other cuts would have to heal in the air.

There was a man working on the front door that Jay Thatcher had broken down. "Just got on his horse and rode out," he said. "Never stopped or looked back."

"Looks like you won all around, Clay," Earl said.

"Did I?"

Earl looked at me curiously and shrugged, giving me a towel to wipe my hands off. Beside me at the table was the packet of belongings Earl had given to me. Idly, I turned it around. Until it hit me.

"What is it, Clay?"

"I don't know . . . something." I opened the package up and went back to that photograph of my father with his company. It was Jake beside him. Wearing sergeant's stripes, as was my pa. And to the left, his face half hidden in the shadow of his hat brim was a man wearing captain's bars. I stared at it numbly, feeling as if my sides had fallen out. Angrily, I slammed my hand to the table.

"Clay?"

"That man," I said. I put my finger on the Captain's image staring blankly back from the old tintype. It was Yule DeLong!

"Who is he?" Earl asked, peering over my shoulder.

"The Captain. A man who served in the army with

my father. The man who had commanded Jake Wadell in the War between the States. The man who was to go into business with Pa. The man who showed up suddenly in Montana after Pa had been killed. Earl," I said looking up, "I think that all of this . . . every mile, every day has been a mistake. The answer is still in Colorado."

TWENTY-ONE

———◆◆———

It was the third day of April when I left Port Keyes, Oregon, on a well-muscled Appaloosa pony Earl had given me. It was the fourteenth of May when the trail-gaunted pony carried me into Denver. The faces of the men on the street were hard, heavy, and whiskered. Most of them were miners, with here and there a solitary prospector still to be found. Then there were those who followed the mines, skimming what gold or silver there was without ever lifting a pick—the gamblers, saloon keepers, bullies, hold-up and hold-out artists, prostitutes, and salesmen of whatever there was to be bought. An occasional Ute or Arapaho, looking lost and out of place in this boom town, stood on the corners, wearing that stoic countenance reserved for white eyes. Not that the Indian was humorless or without hatred or anger, but he had long since learned that any of these expressions of emotion was liable to be misinterpreted, sometimes intentionally so by the white, and so he hid behind his wooden face.

I swung down from the Appy in front of the White Peaks stable and made sure that he was rubbed well before buying him an extra scoop of oats and a hundred pounds of good alfalfa hay.

"Long ride," the hosteler said idly. I nodded and

caught a peek at myself in a fragment of mirror. Naturally thin in the face, my cheeks were absolutely hollow, bushed with a short, curly dark beard. The scars I had picked up courtesy of Jay Thatcher had not yet healed and still carried a raw, pink coloration. My clothes were torn and trail grimed.

"Where's the first place a man can get a bath?"

"Try Long's. First hotel to the left."

I thanked him with a tip and went out. It was a cool night, dark with the scattered clouds hiding the crisp stars. Behind me there was a fight between four miners. They weren't serious about it, being just drunk and high-spirited, but they stirred up considerable dust and cussed more than a middling bit.

I dropped into Long's, and passed over two dollars for a room with a bath. It was upstairs and I hung my gun and climbed into the tub, the hot water relaxing me instantly. A boy with a five-gallon pot kept it hot.

First I would find this Anna Schumann, which should be easy, and make sure that Wind on the Waters was doing all right. Then I would find my old friend, Yule DeLong, and perhaps we would find which of us had learned best how to make a Colt sing and dance. There was a knock.

"Come in!" I half turned to face the opening door, but all I saw was a big hand, a flash of a gun barrel, and a silver star.

"Get up and get dressed."

"Who the hell are you?"

"Dove Haggerty—sheriff of Denver. You're under arrest, Clay Rourke, for robbery."

Dripping wet, I pulled on my pants and boots. No sooner had I stamped into these than I was pushed out the door and down the hallway, the other roomers staring at me as I was muscled forward.

"I don't get this. I haven't even been in town an hour."

"We work fast," Dove said. A steely-eyed, bulky man with two fingers missing on his left hand, a dirty collar and a twitch, he had seen his share of fighting. He struck me as no kind of man to tangle with, so I went along peacefully.

"Throw him in, Ernie."

A sleepy-looking deputy got slowly to his feet and picked the key ring off the wall.

"I don't know what this is about," I protested.

"No?" At that Dove Haggerty's hand stretched out and yanked from my neck the ring I had worn there since Mexico. "The boy pouring your bath water recognized this. Belongs to Mrs. Garr Winkles. There was a sketch of it in the papers for a long time after it was taken from her out in San Francisco. I guess the kid'll get himself a nice reward out of this. And you—I expect you'll get yourself ten years, boy."

"But I never . . ." the excuse caught in my throat. What explanation, after all, could I give? Where was I in from? The coast. Had I been in San Francisco? Yes. Where did I get the ring? What could I say—from a Mexican bandit leader I rode with?

The door closed heavily and the deputy nodded amiably. "Guess you bought it this time, boy. Garr Winkles is a judge hereabouts. You stuck up the wrong coach when you took that."

Justice came quickly in Colorado. The sentence— eight years at hard labor in the Colorado Territorial Prison. The guards were waiting as the judge dropped the gavel. Two men in gray suits, both with wide-brimmed hats. They had a set of irons in their hands.

"Loosen them arms, pal," the older one said.

"I won't wear shackles."

"You'll wear 'em."

Sheriff Dove Haggerty in his court best wandered over to watch.

"I won't wear shackles. Not unless you kill me." I looked steadily into their faces. "I'll go along to prison peacefully, but I won't wear slave irons unless you knock my head in."

"We'll jest do that for ya then," the older one said, lifting a lead-weighted club.

"Jeff." It was Dove Haggerty that spoke. "Let the man alone. I believe him when he says he'll go quiet."

"Dove, it's regulations."

"For me?"

"All right," he sighed with exasperation. "I guess I owe you, Dove. But hold a job open for me. The warden hears about this and I'm liable to get fired."

I couldn't figure Dove Haggerty out. He was a hard one, and positive in his work, yet he had stepped in here. "Thanks, sheriff."

"Do me a favor—when you get out, stay out of Denver," he said gruffly. Then he did a heel turn and strode out of the courtroom.

They put me in the back of a wagon and we headed north the ten miles to the prison, winding through the pleasant grass covered foothills. I could see the Rockies digging at the ceiling of heaven as we made our way, still snow covered, regal, and aloof. I could see a thousand scenes invisible from where I sat. High pine forest, peaceful mountain meadows, the clear rills of spring melt running over the clean granite of the streambed . . . I saw them in my mind, but I had no way of knowing when . . . if, I would ever see them again with my own free eyes.

The Territorial Prison rested on a low mesa, the timber and brush cleared around it for a distance of a thousand yards. A man running across that clearing would have no chance. In the four turrets at the corners of the massive stone building, guards with field glasses and Jaeger target rifles perched.

The guard hopped off the wagon and entered a small door next to the main gate. After a minute he emerged and the gate creaked open, drawn by iron chains. The wagon passed through into the empty courtyard and I was home.

They had said hard labor—and they weren't kidding. There was some road building going on, roadbeds built over rock crushed by twelve-pound sledge hammers. I worked for a time cutting timber which was drawn down by mules for bridges, and then later in the sawmill, planing the same timbers. In the long winters we found ourselves longing for that labor. For it was then we sat and froze and waited . . .

We waited for the same thing, every man-jack of us. The day we would be released or pardoned or see an open door to freedom—a sleepy guard, a loose strand of barbed wire, or a gun thrown through the window. There were crazy moments filled with lunatic schemes and wishes—perhaps there would be a hurricane, an earthquake, an invasion by hostile Indians, a general pardon—ideas that could only find sustenance in utterly desperate minds.

Then, too, we thought of revenge.

I indulged in it on nights when I strained to see the moon from my bunk but could not crane my neck far enough, and only caught the reflected yellow glow through the window where it traced the bars on the floor.

I had been there two years when the wagon rolled up, and I went with the others to see what sort of human cargo had been brought up from the courthouse.

There was a tall, black-suited man with chains locked double, whom someone identified as Tate Locklear, the gunfighter; and a squat, perspiring man in a business suit. Besides these two there was only a couple of ragged, dirty Indians. Yet one of them looked familiar.

I watched as they hobbled, in chains, toward the warden's office where they would have their hair cut, be dressed down, and entered on the rolls. Something . . . Polecat!

It was Polecat; I was sure of it as he vanished behind a low tool shed.

"Polecat! Polecat!"

I gripped the bars to my cell tightly and pressed my head against them, yelling until I was hoarse and one of the guards, his face impassive, shook my shoulder and drew me away.

It was a week before I saw Polecat again, and two weeks before I had the chance to speak to him. We were shoveling coal, laying up for winter once more when I saw the Bow-Piegan working a mule-drawn dray loaded down with coal. Our eyes caught immediately and I nodded to him, but we had to wait for the lunch hour to talk, as silence was the rule.

"Old friend." I was unable to say more at first. I put my hand behind his neck and drew his head to me, slapping his shoulder. He looked hale, but older.

"Clay Rourke—I cannot believe it. We thought you were dead. We were certain! You never came back.

We wrote to Earl even after we left Port Keyes to live with the Schumanns."

"You sound . . . different, Polecat."

"I am different, Clay. It was a strange world I followed you to. The girl and I . . ." he glanced hesitantly at me. "Wind on the Waters."

"But where is she!"

"Then you do care. I did not know what to think. She was only a girl. Now she is a woman, Clay. A fine proud . . . white . . . woman. You would not know her."

"Then everything has gone well for her, at least." I picked up a few lumps of coal and idly shagged them against the wheels of a nearby wagon.

"Well? Yes," he hesitated, "she has become what Anna Schumann wished, educated, cultured as they say."

"But you, Polecat?"

"I am Indian. I was too old to be anything new. I tended the horses for the carriages, dressed in fine livery. I had a dry room, good food; I was treated well."

"But you went away?"

"Yes, Clay. I could not change. One day I folded my clothes and put on my buckskins, taking a knife and wire for snares, and I returned to the mountains to trap, to sleep under the open sky. You see how it was?"

"There's no finer life."

"But there was trouble there too. Three whites wanted my pelts and when they tried to steal them from me I shot one. This man was well known in Leadville. A thief, but a well-known thief." He shrugged. "And so I am here.

"I will show you something," he said as the bell

rang and we trooped back to our work. From his inside pocket he took a newspaper clipping which he handed to me without comment.

There was a picture of a young and beautiful woman there, her hair stacked intricately on top of her fine head with a strand of pearls woven into its dark lustre. She wore a diamond pendant and a ball gown and flashed a perfect, ingenuous smile for the photographer.

> Wendy Waters, Denver's debutante jewel announced her betrothal to Count Wolfgang Hoffholzen of Bavaria. Miss Waters is the protégé of Mrs. Anna Schumann, Herr Hoffholzen's cousin. . . .

I glanced up, but Polecat had gone. Wendy Waters. Engaged to a nobleman, walking in society's company. I was proud of the girl, happy for her . . . but there was a hollowness deep inside me that returned each time I thought of that clipping which I did for the rest of the day and far into the night.

"They will be married next month," Polecat said when I next saw him.

"What?"

"Next month. Wendy . . . Wind on the Waters will marry this German."

"Is he a good man?"

"A good man? Yes," he pondered, "I suppose so. A little stiff, proud of his breeding, but honorable." He watched me, expecting me to say something.

"It has worked out fine for her," I muttered.

"She still talks about you," Polecat confided.

"Whatever I meant to her is gone. It was a child's heart I captured."

"Not to her," he said so solemnly that I nearly believed him. "Even now, if she knew you lived . . ."

"She won't find out!" I snapped angrily.

"You could write."

"Write?" I laughed at the idea. And what would I write? Come back to me, wait for me. Soon I will be out of prison. Give all of that up.

"Polecat, I have nothing for the girl. I wasted my years, learning nothing, accomplishing nothing while she grew and was shaped, educated. Why would I ruin her life, even if I could?"

Even so it gnawed at me while I tried to work and sleep. As if I knew her at all—this new Wendy Waters, the debutante. I forced it from my mind. I would remain where I was for five more long years. By then she would have children, possibly have moved abroad, become only a distant pleasant memory.

And so I worked and sweated, trying to lose myself in my labor, thinking of nothing but the next shovelful of coal, the next wagonload of logs. When I saw Polecat, I said nothing. He obviously thought I was wrong.

"Rourke!"

It was awhile before I heard the voice through my thoughts. I looked up to see the assistant warden, a yellow-skinned man named Yawkey.

"Yes, sir?"

I was bare-chested and the sweat rolled from my face and chest and was stained with the coal dust. He winced as if offended by the sight of me and beckoned me forward with a finger.

"Come with me."

I snatched up my shirt and followed him to the warden's office. Behind the low desk, Warden Lewellan sat smoking a fat cigar. He fingered a sheaf of papers.

"Clay Rourke?"

"Yes, sir!"

He looked me up and down and wagged his head. "You seem to have some enemies, Mister Rourke."

"Sir?"

"I say you have enemies."

"About the same as most folks, I guess. I've crossed some tracks."

"Big tracks, it seems."

I waited while he read the papers again and grumbled as he lost the tube of ash from his cigar on his pants.

"Seems you didn't steal this ring," he said so abruptly I nearly jumped out of my skin. "Leastwise not from Mrs. Garr Winkles. Seems she talks in her sleep or under some other influence. She confessed to her husband, the judge, that she'd been put up to claiming this was her ring."

He slapped the ring on his desk. That same ruby ring I had gotten from Pedro years ago.

"Judge Winkles is a hard man, Rourke. He has to be, here, now. But he's fair. He's signed this release request."

"Wait a minute . . . this is too fast. Mrs. Winkles admitted that this isn't her ring!" I had honestly thought it might have been. Who knew where the Thatcher brothers had gotten that fortune in the first place? From smugglers, petty thieves, buyers of opium, their flunkies.

"It's not hers. She admitted it. Seems some friends of hers . . . do you know Anna Schumann?" the warden asked, lifting a heavy eyebrow.

"No. Only by name."

"Seems she knows you the same way. It seems she was waiting for you to hit town. Those two pillars of society had planned to have you arrested. It was fate that you were carrying that ring. Then, of course, they had something to pin on you. What have they got against you, Rourke?"

"I don't know." But I did. Anna Schumann never wanted me to see her Wendy Waters again. I suppose the girl had talked about me too much. "But three years. Three years!"

"It's the ring did it. I suppose they would have had you arrested for vagrancy or blackmail—who knows? But the kid remembered that robbery on the coast back a few years and went running to Mrs. Winkles." The warden paused. "Like I say, you make enemies."

I stood there numbly, not knowing what to say. Finally, I did ask. "Then I'm free to go?"

"I never said that."

"But you said the judge . . . !"

"He ordered your release from the Denver Territorial Prison, Rourke."

"Then, I don't understand."

"There's a claim in on you. A man's been waiting for you. He wanted you three years ago, but Colorado took precedence. Now we've got to allow your extradition." The warden shook his head again, wearily. "Show him in, Yawkey."

The assistant nodded and opened the door. I turned to see him there.

Marshal Jack Kesselring.

"Howdy, Rourke." His face was twisted with glee. Or was it madness? "Ready for a long ride? Yuma's waiting for you."

"Kesselring, I never . . ."

"No. You never did nothing, did you, Rourke?

Funny how you keep a-landin' in jail and ridin' with outlaws. Them papers ready, warden? I mean to be in Arizona by the first."

The warden handed over the papers and relighted his cold cigar. "The boy makes enemies," I heard him say as Kesselring snapped on the handcuffs and closed the door behind us.

TWENTY-TWO

———◆———

"Look," I told Kesselring, "I don't know where Contreras is now."

"That's been your story all along, Rourke. But now I got you. You'll talk or you'll pay—big. And legal."

We were still in the corridor outside the warden's office. My mind turned over quickly, trying to work an angle loose.

"But I know someone who does know Contreras and where his hideout is. A member of his gang."

"Then we'll find him and talk to him."

"Wait." I brushed his hands off me. "We don't have to find him. He's here in the prison. That's how I know."

"A member of the gang besides you? Here?"

"Sure—an old compadre. Man called Polecat. An Indian who rode plenty with Contreras."

Uncertainly Kesselring's mind rolled that over.

"But I got you, Rourke," he said slowly, "and you know too."

"It's been four years. They've moved the hideout," I told him, shrugging as innocently as I could. His eyes were uncertain now.

"There's a way, isn't there?" I asked him.

"Maybe—but why are you so helpful all of the sudden?"

"I figured I'd better be," I told him. That he could understand and he nodded with grim satisfaction.

"We could spring this Injun. I'd have to say I had a bill on him in Arizona. He wanted there?"

"I don't think so."

"That makes it rougher. Sometimes a man's wanted down there we make an exchange. Hand over the reward money to the arresting body. But there ain't a reward, you say?"

"Not an official one."

"What d'you mean?"

"If it would help . . . I've got a ring that's almighty valuable in my left shirt pocket. Warden seemed to shine to it, and it's not stolen merchandise. He knows it's not."

"Maybe this warden don't go for that kinda stuff."

"You're a lawman, aren't you?"

"It'd be bending things a mite," Kesselring said, but I could see the idea had hooked him.

"You bend—maybe they'll bend. It's a matter of custody, anyway. Not like you were trying to free the man."

But I was, and desperately. I watched as Kesselring's slow mind pondered the proposition point by point. "Gimme the ring—we'll see."

Polecat joined us in the courtyard and we rode from the territorial prison, wearing cuffs, with Marshal Kesselring's rifle muzzle prodding us south, toward Arizona. Warden Lewellan waved us a warm fare-the-well.

"This man," Polecat said without looking at me. "He is not well."

"He's obsessed," I agreed. "This idea of revenge for his brothers has driven him mad. I think it's five years now he's been tracking Contreras."

We rode easily, silently for the most part, following the twisting whims of the South Platte River. The air was pure and fragile, unlike the heavy prison air I was used to. The larks and red-winged blackbirds trilled in the tall, scented grass. There was a warm drowsiness to it all. Except . . . I could have sworn there was someone following us. Once I caught a reflection of sunlight where none should have been, unless it was a small pool or a metallic rock, but I had seen no quartz or mica, or anything like that in passing. There was something else. Call it instinct. Maybe the way the shadows moved in the trees that day; something did not feel right, and I had been in the wilderness too often not to trust that sixth sense, which is after all only a subconscious awareness of clues which are too subtle for our conscious mind to register as warnings.

Kesselring's mood had grown sour. His eyes were blank, but he frequently made bitter comments about "killers," "bandits," and other that were unintelligible. We camped just a mile out of Denver, the lights from the town casting a whitish halo against the starless black sky.

"How long do you think I'll wait?" Kesselring said abruptly over his coffee cup.

"What?"

"You! Injun Joe. How long do you think I'll wait? I want you to do some talking about Contreras." He was watching Polecat hard, his Winchester across his lap.

"I've gotten you into something," I said in a low voice.

"I'll take you there," Polecat bluffed. "Once we are in Arizona."

"You will. That you will." He was coldly quiet.

The handcuffs we still wore chafed our wrists. I asked Kesselring to take them off, but he just laughed. "I been in this business fifteen years, Rourke. Found out that I'd rather have a sore-armed prisoner than a bullet in the head. Can't argue with that, can you?"

"Maybe you will let Rourke go," Polecat suggested. "I will take you to Contreras."

"No, I'll go along," I objected.

"He goes," Kesselring said, throwing out the dregs of his coffee. "Or I kill him. I'm taking no chance on having a man loose behind me." Kesselring stood and without warning he swept at Polecat with his rifle butt, catching him on the temple. Polecat went sprawling, the blood raining from his forehead. I came to my feet but Kesselring had his rifle on me.

"Sit down!" He was panting as he spoke. "Now, Injun Joe, I told you to start talking. Did you think I was talking to hear myself talk?"

Bitterly, I cursed myself for getting Polecat into this. What could he tell the marshal? Nothing. And even a bluff was bound to be detected. And Kesselring was ready to kill. I could see it in him. Polecat managed to roll to his knees, and he lifted his face. He nodded. "Okay, I'll tell you."

"That's better."

"There is a camp on a high mesa . . ."

"What mesa?"

"Just over the border. There are pine trees."

"Pine trees!" Kesselring laughed hard for a brutal moment and then, striking like a snake, he clubbed Polecat again, this time nearly knocking him unconscious.

"The first pine tree I see in Baja I'll eat my horse raw! Now talk straight, Injun Joe. Or you're going to die."

It was utterly silent. The flames from our low fire painted Kesselring's savage face. The frogs along the dark riverbanks chortled and a fish splashed. The night was taut and I was sweating. I had brought my friend out of prison to be killed! Poor Polecat could not imagine a land where no pine trees decorated majestic mountains—the desert, if he had heard of it, was a myth to his mountain-bred intelligence as far distant and unimaginable as the surface of the bleak moon.

Kesselring sat down again on the flat rock. He watched as Polecat struggled to his feet. Calmly the marshal spoke to him. "No matter. I guess you'll talk after we get to Yuma."

"Yes. Yes, I will," Polecat promised. "I'll talk to you there."

"Good." Kesselring poured a cup of coffee and handed it over to Polecat. "And if not in Yuma, well, by the time we get down to the border, to Phoenix, you'll surely have your memory back."

"Yes," Polecat said numbly, "surely by then."

My eyes were frozen on Kesselring. He had set the hook and hard.

"Phoenix ain't on the border, Injun Joe. And if you ever been to Arizona, you know we'll hit Phoenix before we hit Yuma. Injun Joe, you been lyin' to me. You, too, Rourke. I don't think Injun Joe knows a thing. I think he's extra baggage." Then Kesselring, without hesitation, levered a bullet into the chamber and fired, the bellow of his rifle shattering the night. I saw Polecat spin and go down, blood staining his shirt and I threw myself at the marshal. He tried to chop at me with the rifle barrel but missed. I grabbed for the Winchester, but in handcuffs I couldn't do much and he rolled aside, coming up with the rifle dead on me, his hair in his face. His jaw was set, his eyes wide and white.

"I ought to kill you too, Rourke, for tricking me."

"Wait."

"Wait, hell," he snapped and his rifle went to his shoulder, aimed directly at Polecat who was already down, writhing in pain. His gun exploded, but so did the rifle from the woods and Kesselring, looking at me questioningly, and then at his rifle, toppled over. He was dead, a neat, smoldering hole directly over his heart.

It had been a time, but I knew the man who had shot Kesselring as soon as he stepped into the camp circle. The firelight, flickering in the slight breeze clearly illuminated the substantial features of Jake Wadell. The repeater in his hand was still smoking. He looked at me, grunted, and levered home a fresh cartridge.

TWENTY-THREE

———◆◆———

"Here." Jake tossed the rifle to me and I caught it without thinking. "There's a hay wagon parked up along the main road. We best borrow it and get the Indian to a doctor. Piegan, ain't he?" he said, peering closely at Polecat. "Long ways from home . . . I'll get that wagon."

I put the rifle down, curious as I was, I was concerned more with Polecat's condition. There was a nasty-looking hole through his upper shoulder. The collarbone looked to be broken and maybe the shoulder blade as well. I bound him tightly and gave him water which he kept asking for, even after he had finished the quart canteen.

"Where's the nearest house?" I asked him.

"House? Schumann house—take me there. In my room I have good herbs. Schumann house."

"All right." It was the last place I wanted to go, but there was no time to be thinking about my feelings. I could hear the wagon coming and in a moment Jake appeared, his horse hitched to the rig. We placed Polecat carefully in the back. I rode with him while Jake headed toward the big house in the long valley.

"Kesselring?" Polecat wanted to know.

"Dead. Jake killed him to protect us. Though I don't know why."

Jake looked around at me but said nothing.

"He was a man gone mad."

"He couldn't give it up," I said as the wagon rocked along. "He wanted Contreras so bad he could see nothing else, think of nothing else. He should have given it up years ago, this hunting. He chased after death until he caught it."

"And you, friend," Polecat said softly. "What of your chase, Clay Rourke? Will it end any differently?"

There was nothing I could say to that. The big house loomed ahead, the lights glaring from the windows. Long colonnades of aspen, dark in the moonless night, stood sentinel along the entranceway. There were carriages in front, many of them. The Schumanns were entertaining apparently.

"My room—at the back, behind the stable, Clay."

Jake pulled to the back of the big house and we found Polecat's small room, empty since he had not stayed there for a time, but there were blankets in the closet and his beaverskin pouch was filled with herbs.

"You will boil these?" he asked, handing me a handful of dry, brownish leaves which I thought were yarrow. I took them and did as he asked. We watched as Polecat made his own poultice and then, exhausted, fell back to sleep.

We had the small lantern lit, the smoky glow filling the room except for the corners which stayed dark and were filled with cobwebs. I watched Jake Wadell fill a pipe and light it. He turned slowly to me knowing I had questions.

"I guess we should talk."

"I'd say so."

"Sergeant Wadell, wasn't it—when you knew my father first?"

"It was," he affirmed with a quick shake of his head.

"And it was Captain DeLong . . . or Hewitt still."

"Yes. We were together in the army. Yule, Bolen, Trollis Bake Jepitt, and Free Wyler—we came west together to Colorado after the war. All of us, like we was still in the army. Following the Captain—De-Long. He had to change his name from Hewitt after some trouble in El Paso.

"We tried a little of this and that. Tried a bank at Trinidad, a coach or two," Jake said, stroking his black beard. "Finally, we decided to go into the cattle business. So we started stocking them up in the hills. They wore every brand in the register, but those cows didn't seem to mind changing locale. It got easy—too easy. Finally old Dove Haggerty started to cut us off."

"I've met the sheriff. He's a goer."

"He is," Jake agreed. "They started lookin' for our hole and we had to keep pushin' those cows further up into the hills. Finally, it occurs to the Captain—DeLong—that your pappy had him a place in Montana. But your pappy didn't hold with such goings on. That's why he never rode west with us after the war. DeLong thought he could talk your pa into it, but he discovered he'd have to kill him to get that ranch up there."

"Then he meant to drive the stolen cattle to Montana."

"Right. About you we knew nothing."

"It's incredible. And brutal, Jake. Why are you talking now? Why were you in Port Keyes? That was you, wasn't it?"

"I thought you saw me," he laughed, slapping his

thick knee. "I rode out because I saw DeLong pick up with you. I didn't want him killing you—you saved my life, Clay. Saved it when I was your enemy. Though I never would've killed your daddy."

"Why didn't DeLong kill me? He could have."

"Maybe. There was the Indian with you, though," he reminded me, nodding to Polecat. "And besides— he knew you were heading to the coast, out of the picture. That's why he rode that far with you, I reckon. To make sure."

"But he actually gave me money!" I got to my feet, waving my hands in disbelief, "And even taught me to shoot."

"That'd be Yule DeLong for you. He felt sorry for you, so he gave you money. He liked you, so he taught you to shoot. Hell, Clay, he liked your daddy—he told me so many times. He said—I sure hate like hell to kill Rourke."

"Then why . . . ?"

"That's the sort of man the Captain is. Notional. He was raised on a big plantation in the south. As a boy he was taught that whatever he wanted was right. He never unlearned that lesson. He'd feel sorry for a fellow as he robbed him and knocked his head in. But he'd sure as hell do it if he thought he had to."

"I can't even understand that sort of man."

"There's many of 'em, Clay. You've seen a bit of the world now, and you ought to know it."

"And now? Now, Jake—where is he?"

"You're not through with him?" he asked, raising his thick black eyebrows.

"No! I'm not through by a damn sight."

"He'll kill you—I never saw a man so good with a gun. Or so cold with its use."

"He'll kill me then! But I'll try him, Jake—I'll try

him." I leaned across the table, my face set, and I locked eyes with Jake Hewitt, this bad man, and he saw it there. I would do it, and I might even have a chance at winning.

"He's in Montana. Living on your ranch. Has been for five years, Clay." Jake stuffed his cold pipe into his pocket and stood up. "Those stolen cows have dropped their calves and by now they're full grown beeves wearing a legal DeLong brand. I imagine he's doing well. And not a stolen cow left on the range, I'd bet. All butchered out long ago. He's gotten away with it."

"No. He hasn't yet."

Jake was standing over Polecat and I joined him. The Piegan's face was clammy and cold. The bullet wound had a nasty red cast to it. The poultice, probably cleansing and healing in the woods for a cut or scrape, was doing nothing for the infection of a bullet or for the shock. Jake spoke my own thoughts.

"Them leaves ain't gonna set no busted bones. He's in bad shape—probably bone splinters too. He needs some professional work. A doctor."

"Then I'll ride into Denver and get the doctor." I picked up my hat and moved toward the door.

"He's not in town," Jake said. "Doc Corson was invited to this shindig of Anna Schumann's. There some big politicos from Mexico visiting, including Fuentes, the vice-president. Everyone in Denver that could get an invitation is in the house."

I stopped cold in my tracks. That meant I would have to go up there. And there was more than one person there I didn't wish to see. And at least one I would be embarrassed to see me. Polecat was suffering; I nodded to Jake and went out.

*   *   *

It was dry and cold, the sounds of muted laughter and the muffled strains of music came from the big white house where all was light and gay. I walked across the neatly planted flower gardens and went up to the front.

"Hello, Rourke."

My head jerked up. It was Dove Haggerty. Lounging on the porch, he was obviously not a member of the party, but more than likely a paid watchdog.

"Sheriff."

"Heard you were released," he said with an amiable nod. "Glad for you."

"Thanks," I replied. I waited for him to ask what my business was here, but he didn't say a word. His eyes were inscrutable under the shadow cast by his flat-brimmed hat. Maybe he assumed I was there to talk to the Schumann woman, but whatever his thoughts were he said nothing, although his eyes swept down me, noticing the ill-fitting clothing, the dust and torn shirt.

Maybe it was simply that he saw I had no gun. He let me go on by, and I entered the brilliant white world of the Schumann house where everything was chenille and silk, crystal and silver. Men in red sashes spoke in low voices to ladies in gowns that trailed the floor. Their heads came up as I pushed past.

"Doctor Corson?" I asked, grabbing a butler by the elbow.

"Over there," he said in a haughty way. I guess I looked like I had need of the doctor, though, and he let me go by unchallenged as well.

"Corson?"

The little silver-haired man looked up from his glass. "Yes, I'm Corson."

"I've a badly hurt friend around back in the garden house."

"I really can't . . ."

"You really can! I said he's bad off."

As I raised my voice heads turned around. A lady whispered behind her fan. Over to the corner I saw a cluster of Mexican gentlemen, and with them, looking uncomfortable in their tight suits a couple of men who looked like *vaqueros* misplaced—bodyguards I took them for. There was a proud-looking fellow with long whiskers and a row of medals. That would be the vice-president of Mexico, Fuentes.

"What's going on here?"

It was Judge Garr Winkles and he recognized me. He winced like he had been slapped and a sheepish look spread slowly across his face. It was his wife had framed me over that ring, and he who had sentenced me unjustly. Maybe he thought I was looking for him.

"Got an injured man, judge," I said. "We need the doctor."

"Well, Doc," Winkles said, "you got a customer, looks like."

I looked at the judge and nodded just slightly. Maybe he knew I was supposed to be on my way to Arizona in custody, but probably he didn't. That seemed to be a sideline of the warden alone, trading prisoners for reward money. At any rate, he was contrite enough that he wished me no more ill will.

I heard the bustling of skirts and up came Anna Schumann. She was a little short, with a sharp, pointed nose and a slightly long neck. She sniffed a little as she caught sight of me standing there—a big, rough-looking man I was, in rough clothing with a hard cast to my eyes. But she knew me, or thought she did, and her breath caught just for a second.

"Who's injured?" she asked, peering through her lorgnette, those glasses on a stick.

"Polecat, ma'm."

"Polecat . . . I don't . . . the Indian fellow?"

Folks had gathered around us, including a few of those *vaqueros* and the vice-president. I was embarrassing Anna Schumann, and I knew it, but it couldn't be helped. The vice-president was right next to me and beside him was a man I knew. A man from a long way back.

"Yes, ma'm. The Indian fellow."

"It's up to you, doctor, of course," she said. "Can you trust this man?"

I didn't mean to cause such a stir. That party must've been awfully boring the way they all gathered around to see the excitement. I noticed this tall blond fellow with a European look to him and cold blue eyes, with one of those dueling scars on his cheek. I knew him without ever having seen him. Wolfgang Hoffholzen. The man who would marry . . . and she was just beside him. Her black eyes wide, her mouth slightly open. Hesitantly, she stepped forward then stopped.

"Wendy," Anna Schumann said, "that Indian fellow has been injured. The one who used to work here. You remember."

"Polecat!" Wind on the Waters said and her hand went to her throat. If she hadn't been sure before, she was sure now. It was me she saw and not an apparition. "Where is he, Clay? Dr. Corson, won't you come immediately. Count," she said to Hoffholzen, "please excuse me. I assure you this is a dire emergency. I'll return soon."

"I'll come along," he said.

"No!"

"But I insist, Wendy," Hoffholzen snapped. He stiffened a little and eyed me like he'd seen his first rattler.

"Please, no," she said, putting a restraining hand on his.

"But this man . . ." he said, waving a hand at me as he looked for a word to describe me.

"He's an old friend," Wendy replied. "Excuse me, Señor Fuentes. Anna . . . I must go. Doctor, are you ready?"

"Yes." The butler had given Corson his bag and hat and he was already following Wendy toward the door. I waited a second, surveying the scene, feeling like a fox loose in the hound kennel.

Jake let us in. Astonished, he eyed Wind on the Waters, then backed away to the corner. The doctor was already unwrapping the dressing. "Not bad," he said under his breath. Once away from the party he was all business. "Not good, but not bad. I'd like some hot water, please, and some clean cloths. Miss Waters, can we obtain some clean linen?"

After getting what the doctor needed there was nothing else for us to do. Wendy and I stood by, not looking at one another. Finally, I muttered some excuse and went out.

I could still hear the music, and from there I could see the lights playing on the river down near Denver. There was a cool breeze, shaking the birds in the golden aspen. It was nearly midnight and now the cold orange moon was rising. I turned to a hand on mine.

"You came back."

She was just looking at me, her eyes dark and liquid in the early moonlight and I felt my face go hot. She was shorter than me, coming not quite to my shoulders, and she smelled like the meadows in summer with the coverlets of wild flowers, the ripening grass, and the scent of cedar coming from the high up mountains.

"He'll be all right," I said. Her hand was still on mine.

"Yes."

"I understand . . . this Count Hoffholzen."

"We were to be married. But now!" She pressed in closer to me and I backed off a hair. "You've grown into a strong man, Clay. I can't believe it. You don't know how many nights I've watched out my window for you."

"Wendy—how you've changed."

"No. Not inside. I haven't, Clay." She stepped back, keeping my hands. "Things will be wonderful now. You can stay on with Anna for a while. And then we can find you a position. Anna knows just everybody!"

"I can't just yet. I can't settle. Not here, anyway. My home is in the Milk River country. You know that."

"You want to eke out an existence there! Don't you remember the long, brutal winters? The mornings when the pot is empty and underneath there is no wood to start a fire and so nothing is cooked? For days on end."

"I remember. That's my home, Wendy. What kind of ideas have you been growing up on?"

"Maybe you're right," she said, touching her forehead nervously. "Maybe I could . . . be a squaw again." She laughed tensely and turned her back to me. "For you."

"We'll talk about it. After I'm through."

"Through?" She spun back, her eyes flashing. "Through with what?"

"DeLong. He was the Captain."

"The Captain?" She was confused, then slowly she remembered. "That still! Clay, it's been so long. So long. Let it end. We can be together. Here. Happy."

"No, I can't."

"You are obsessed with it. With killing. All of the brutality has stayed inside of you and been nurtured by the life you've led. Why? Here, we could have everything. Together."

"That is *your* obsession," I said, "I don't know what my life can bring. How it will end. But I won't stop."

"Until you have killed every enemy you've ever had!"

"Wendy, I don't wish it. But there is no law in the north country, or here for that matter. None that can reach beyond the territorial borders, none that can catch these wanton killers. Out here it is a man alone who provides justice."

"Like a savage!"

"Just like a savage," I responded softly. I understood her. What person does like hatred, killing, brutality, but everything I had said was true. Who was there to punish Yule DeLong but me?

She was soft and without warning she turned her softness to me, her lips pliable and warm met mine and she kissed me briefly but intensely, her arms around my waist. Then she leaned her head against my chest. She was crying, I thought, but softly.

"Wendy! A voice called, carrying across the garden. It was Hoffholzen. Wendy hesitated a moment and then pushed away, kissing my hand.

"I have to go to him. I have to tell him something."

"Maybe you'd better wait."

"Too much has waited." She was nearly invisible in the darkness of the shadows cast by the trees, but the glow of the paling moon caught her fine features in the hollows of her cheeks and glittered in her soft eyes.

"There's more. I have to fight."

"In Montana, yes." She sniffed and gripped my hand tighter yet. "I understand. We'll face it when we have to."

"Wendy!" Hoffholzen called again, this time closer.

"Not in Montana," I said sharply. "Here."

"No. Not in Anna's house," she pleaded.

"Wendy!" The German was looking for us on every pathway.

"Here." I pushed her hands from me. "I must fight him here."

"No!" She stood trembling. "You like it!" She stared at me numbly. "You like it, Clay Rourke! Killing. Bloodshed. You enjoy it."

"I don't . . ."

"You have fought all of your life. Except for the one time I would have had you fight for me."

"Yellow Glove . . ."

"Yellow Glove would have killed you, perhaps. But that would have been for me."

"And that would excuse it? It seems it is always excusable when it is for oneself. But you were a girl. A child. I did not want you. Not for a wife."

"Now . . . ?" Wendy's eyes opened suddenly. Behind her was Hoffholzen, his back stiff with rage, his blond hair across his brow, a pistol in his hand.

"Go on, Wendy," I told her. "We can't make up for

the lost years in a few minutes. Go back to your Anna Schumann, your parties. Now there is a man I must kill."

Hoffholzen stood there quietly, his hands trembling with anger; the pistol he carried loose in his hand came up to meet me as I stepped forward.

TWENTY-FOUR

———◆→———

"In my country," Count Hoffholzen said in carefully measured, accented tones, "a man does not suffer indignities without recompense. I must ask you to find a weapon and return. Otherwise," he said with a shrug and a glance at Wendy, "I will kill you where you stand, my barbarian friend."

I nodded, shrugged in return and stepped suddenly forward. I took his wrist and forced the pistol from it, bending the hand back on itself. Then I picked it up and cast it into the shadows.

"I'm sorry, sir. I don't have the time for that. Wendy is an old friend of mine. We spoke. If that has offended you, I apologize." Then I pushed by him and started toward the garden house where Polecat lay. Jake stepped out of the shadows as I passed, a rifle in his hands.

"I was watching," he said. "That fellow came busting in lookin' for you. He don't know how lucky he come out. It could've been me and my Winchester. Or worse—he might've found you with a gun on."

"I need your Colt, Jake. I'll bring it back soon. If I can."

He grunted and unbuckled it. I tested the balance of the revolver once and slid it in and out of the holster a couple of times. Then I tied it down and went to the big house.

This time Sheriff Haggerty did want to talk to me, but I was by him so fast there was no time for conversation. I marched square up to the Mexican party where Anna Schumann was being the good hostess. The *vaqueros* got a glimpse of me and one of them produced a derringer from inside his sleeve.

"Again, my young friend," the silver-haired Fuentes said with a twinkle in his eyes. He sipped from his drink, one finger lifted. "Again he needs a doctor," he laughed. "You must work quickly."

"It's not a doctor this time, Señor Fuentes. Not yet. I apologize for intruding again."

"And well you should," Anna Schumann said tautly. "It is outrageous."

"Nearly as outrageous as conspiring to send an innocent man to jail," I said. "I had said nothing of that, realizing you were good to Wendy and that you probably thought you were doing right by her."

I caught a glimpse of Wendy's face. She had rushed in from the garden, her face flushed, in time to hear that.

"But your present business, *señor?*" Fuentes asked. "My *vaqueros*, as you see, are not interested in the past affairs of our hostess, but of your present intentions. I see you are armed."

"I am. Señor Fuentes, I mean to kill a member of your party."

"What—he jests! No. He does not, I see. But who?"

"It is me he means," General Hector Cedeno said stepping forward. "We have met, no?"

"We have. And I see you have prospered since that time."

"You have met?" the vice-president said. "But where?"

"In Puerto La Paloma. I was on board my uncle's ship. The general was adjutant there. General Cedeno was at that time smuggling opium to the United States on my uncle's ships and also raiding towns in the interior of Baja, claiming that Pedro Carnero was responsible."

"General?"

"Absurd, Señor Fuentes. It is absurd."

"I say it is not—you are the liar, general."

The party was in uproar with the mayor, the sheriff, and several citizens trying to keep back a group of angry American dignitaries. Anna Schumann seemed ready to faint. Wendy I did not see.

"You cannot call me a liar," General Cedeno hissed.

"I can. You are."

The vice-president stood apart from it all, faintly amused, it seemed. He motioned to his *vaqueros* to stand back. Cedeno would fight me, and I knew it. Not to fight was cowardice, an acceptance of guilt. He would fight, and if he won there would be no one to accuse him. If I were to kill him at least he would avoid the disgrace of demotion and imprisonment. I thought Fuentes half-believed me. I turned to him.

"If there is a chance, señor, the people of that region should be questioned by delegates from Mexico City. They can tell you that your own army is responsible for abusive acts, rape, looting, blackmail—not Carnero who is an honorable man. When I was in Mexico they said it was Pablo Carillo who misinformed the *presidente*. Perhaps his papers could be examined. But I assure you, I do not lie."

"You are a fool," the general said. He had regained

some of his composure. "A man hears stories and repeats them. It is a shame to die for lies, my friend."

"But not to die for murder and plunder."

"So be it," the general said. "We will fight then. A duel of honor. At the light of the sun." His eyes went to the Colt on my hip and as he turned his back to me he said, "As the injured party I choose sabers with which to settle this."

"I have no saber."

"I have one, señor," the vice-president said. "A fine weapon. And I hope you have the skills necessary to defend yourself with it. For the general is most impressive with a sword. Most impressive."

At that he turned and went out. I lingered a moment longer and walked to the front porch. Sabers! And what did I know of sword fighting? With fists or guns or knives, I had no fear of the man Cedeno. But sabers!

"You bought yourself a packet of trouble, Rourke."

The sheriff was standing by me, his steely eyes unamused.

"Don't I know it."

"Was that true? What you were saying in there?"

"True as death," I said.

"Then I wish you luck, Rourke. From what I've learned of you it hasn't been an easy life for you. You deserve to go on a bit longer."

"Thanks, Dove."

"I heard another rumor," he said slowly. "I hear you mean to go after an old enemy of mine. Yule De-Long."

"Now how . . . ? It's true. If I get the chance."

"You take them in clusters, don't you, kid? Lord, you make some enemies. But take my advice—it's three hours to dawn. If you know somebody that knows something about sabers, you find him, and fast."

Jake was waiting for me around back. Tersely I told him what was happening. He shook his massive head and sucked in his lower lip. "That's bad. You went about it wrong."

"But that's the way it is now."

"Look, Clay, I know something about it. I was in the cavalry with your daddy. Now the saber's chiefly an officer's weapon. They like the looks of 'em, more'n anything else. But I've played with them. But it's been years back now. Years."

He showed me what he could, however. We practiced with a pair of slats. Twice he touched me with his stick and I was beginning to get good and worried. Already the pale glow of false dawn was in the eastern sky. I stood there sweating from the exertion, shaking my head dismally.

"Look," Jake said finally. "I think you're better off using your natural quickness, your reflexes. Don't try at all to fight him the way a fellow is taught, the way these duelists do it in Europe. Just stay away from him, circle, do what you have to to keep him off balance. Fight like what you've got is a long knife and not a dueling sword . . . and do it quick, whatever you do. Do it quick. Or, Clay—he'll cut you in two."

The rose of the dawning sun was opening behind the thick aspen and birch across the river. The grass, where the sun had not yet touched, was white with frost. Our feet made dark circles on it as we walked. It was Dove Haggerty, who walked beside me, carrying my coat and the saber the vice-president had loaned me. Surprisingly, he had offered to be my second.

"Señor." General Cedeno nodded, his face slightly amused. He was in shirt sleeves and dark trousers, a red sash around his waist.

"I am ready," I told him. He smiled as if saying it was not so. I wasn't ready—it was true—but I would have at it.

The vice-president was there in a long coat, breath steaming from his mustached lips as he spoke to the man beside him. He nodded vaguely. Anna Schumann had come as well, though Wendy was absent. She had already made her feelings clear on fighting. Count Hoffholzen was present, and he didn't look any too concerned one way or the other. Dr. Corson, Judge Winkles, and a couple of men I didn't know were there also.

"Gentlemen?"

The general unsheathed his saber and tossed the sheath aside. His sword caught the fire of the morning sun and sparkled with it. My own sword felt heavy, awkward in my hand. The general assumed a dueling position, hand to his hip, legs slightly bent and poised. I touched my blade to his and he lunged forward.

Quickly, catlike, he thrust toward me, his whole body following a learned pattern. His legs were like springs, his blade like an extension of his mind, quick to follow instructions.

The tip of his saber took a bite at my left shoulder. He was smiling, playing with me. His saber danced, striking like a snake and I felt a tug at my shirt low on the right side. A trickle of blood ran into my waistband. For a minute I stood there transfixed, then Jake's voice boomed out.

"Move, Clay! Move!"

Jarred into action, I began to circle. I took a swipe at Cedeno with my saber and then turned it over, holding the blade up like a knife. The general was standing still. He shrugged and shouted to the count.

"Have you, Herr Count, tried to duel a rabbit! Stand still, rabbit, and fight like a man!"

For a minute the taunt stung, and I considered trading thrusts and parries with him, but he had all the skills necessary to win the duel. I wanted only to survive long enough to let him taste my steel.

Like a crow he came suddenly forward in two short hops. His blade whistled past my ear as I pulled away, then spun back and twisted upward from my waist to the left shoulder. My shirt was cut to ribbons and he lunged again, this time coming for the heart. I went to my back and tripped him. He went down with a grunt and I plunged for him.

Now he was mad, his pride ruffled by the tumble. He came quickly to his feet, his hair mussed, shirt dirty, fire in his eyes. There had been a few chuckles in the crowd as this fine swordsman chased me around the circle, but now it was deathly silent. He came forward furiously, his blade cutting arabesques. I ducked, rolled aside, circled, and clumsily beat off his attacks with my sword.

I had no skill, but he was not bringing his to bear either as we fought like savages, swinging and grunting with the effort. I had broken into a sweat and my senses had become honed, locked into this sport which led to death. I anticipated his blows now, noticing the tenseness in his muscles, the way he leaned, even measuring the feints by instinct, detecting how they differed from the real, following thrusts.

A duelist meets another face to face and their

deadly game is programmed, each using certain moves well known to the other and countering in a like manner with certain predictable moves. But we thrust and cut and circled, dodging as we lay steel on the space between us. I went right, then came left, jabbed, and saw for the first time the crimson result of a well-executed blow on the general's shirt.

Furiously, he lay into me, cutting wildly as a pirate in a boarding party. But these were blows I knew— the blows any man uses in angry fighting whether the weapon is sticks or bowie knives or sledge hammers. I blocked a stroke and our sabers clashed as we moved together. I took his wrist as we did so and tossed him to the ground. But the general was up and moving away, his face red and furious at the turn things had taken.

I had no finesse, but I knew fighting and had the will for it.

The day had dawned clear. It seemed my eyes took in everything at once. The sweep of green grass, the white house beyond. The trees, the birds low along the river—all, while I staved off this swordsman. The general was tiring.

It's no easy problem to hold out a saber for a long period of time. No more than it is for a boxer to hold up his arms for the long rounds of fighting, and as in boxing the edge goes ever so slowly over to the stronger man.

His thrusts were slower now, and I moved easily aside. He followed me now too. Chasing me angrily, he cut at the air until his sword arm was weary with the weight.

"Damn you!" he muttered. He was drenched with sweat. His face was pale, slack. We came together again and our swords met at the hilt. Viciously, I drew back my left hand and slammed it into his wind, The general grunted and backed up, doubling over. I touched him again—on the thigh—and he cursed and fell back farther, his leg streaming blood.

He came on again—and again I circled away. Now he was fighting for his pride, his position, his life— and he knew it, and he had found a second wind somewhere. Our sabers clicked and parted, swarming like insects, fluttering in the golden sunlight. And we fought on.

Suddenly he feinted, came across my body and swept up with his sword. It was not the first time he had used this maneuver. The first time he had cut my chest. This time he was slower. This time I saw it coming. This time the saber went in to the hilt, a gush of gore pouring forth from the bowels.

The general, sword in hand, turned to the vice-president and bowed. Then he toppled forward on his face, the angry stinger of my saber poking from his back.

He was utterly silent. The general was dead. I swayed a little on my feet. I was covered with blood— most of it not my own. Dove Haggerty came forward suddenly and put his arm around my waist. Then Jake was there and the doctor. They put me down on a fallen log when I refused to lay on the grass, and I sat there as they bandaged me.

I saw her far across the lawn, standing upstairs on the balcony. Her dark hair was loose on her shoulders. For just a moment she stood there, and then she was gone.

"That girl still loves you," Anna Schumann said with tender disgust. Then she went away, muttering to herself.

"She does, you know," Count Hoffholzen said. "She

told me so last night. May I offer some advice, Mister Rourke? Make sure you choose the weapons next time." Then he tipped his hat and strode away, whistling.

"That true?" Jake asked. "About the girl? Lord, she's a beautiful creature."

I didn't answer him. I didn't know if it were true or not. But if it were true that this woman loved me so much that she had waited these five years for my return—this beautiful, most feminine woman—what kind of man had I become to turn my back on her love to chase after death once more?

Yule DeLong and I would meet again. I would go home to Montana. I knew it even as I sat there bleeding from the morning's combat. The duel with Cedeno had been a fight for friends far distant, for a people I knew for a time and had come to love. A fight for their rights, their land, their freedom.

With Yule DeLong the fight was for what was mine. And I would not be denied that combat.

TWENTY-FIVE

$\bullet\!\!-\!\!\bullet\!\!-\!\!\bullet$

The steel-dust gelding stood saddled and waiting. Polecat sat up with a struggle and took my hand. His shoulder was still heavily bandaged and he apologized.

"I am growing old, Clay. The bones take time to mend. But I will come. I will be coming home. I only regret that I cannot help you now. If you would wait . . ."

"I can't wait. I have waited for five years. Now I must go."

"To kill."

Wind on the Waters was in the doorway, her face drawn, a shawl loose on her shoulders.

"Yes—if I am lucky."

"Clay . . . you could stay. With me. I will ask only this once more."

"Wind on the . . . Wendy," I said. "Maybe that's the trouble. You are no longer Wind on the Waters. And this woman—Wendy Waters—has lived a settled life too long, she forgets how things are where there is no butler, no sheriff, no gathering of friends to protect you.

"Wind on the Waters knew of the sudden and savage attacks by the Gros Ventre, the Blackfoot, yes, and the whites. But you, Wendy, cannot conceive of a band of murderers storming this fine house to kill, loot, and rape. But that is what has happened to my home. I have been attacked, my land has been raped. Land my father fought for, trying to provide a decent home for me. Now it is my blood that must be gambled. I cannot add more . . . if you no longer understand this, we will never understand each other anymore."

She was framed in the soft light of the doorway. Her narrow hands drew her white shawl still tighter as her mouth fluttered, not quite saying anything, before it collapsed into a trembling gasp. She rushed out with a shake of her head and we heard her sobbing as she went.

It tore at my emotions, and at Polecat's. But there was nothing to be done for it. The doorway was an empty frame. Something had been torn from our hearts—something irreplaceable and fine. I took Polecat's hand again, briefly, and left, stepping into the steel-dust's saddle without looking back. I turned his long head northward, following the South Platte for ten lazy miles before drifting west toward the great bulky spine of the Great Divide.

Twenty-one days later we forded the Upper Missouri near Camas Meadows and came into Montana, and suddenly a great feeling welled up inside me. I was home to the broad green grasslands, the icy blue waters of its sweet running rivers, the broad, crystal sweep of its blue skies—the big land, my land.

It was at Fort Ellis that I first saw the Long "D" brand. Yule DeLong. They were penned up in the army stockyard, about twenty fat, sleek head of longhorn, sired out of some shorthorn bull, what I couldn't tell—all that shorthorn stuff was new to me. But the beef these steers carried was heavy on their frames, and I'll give it to DeLong, he knew his breeding.

"That one there's for Sunday pot roast," a straw-chewing sergeant told me. "Nice-looking stuff ain't they? Used to be our cows were drove all the way from Kansas. Stringy? Man, them cows was rough eating! These here are Montana bred, believe it or smile. Only about three spreads doing it yet, but it's the coming thing."

"That's what my daddy always thought," I remarked.

"Yeah—well, my daddy always told me there was gold in California, but he never went. It's the doers that have, stranger. Your daddy should have got him some of that range like the Long 'D' 's got."

"Yeah. He should have."

"Well, maybe you will, someday."

"I might," I acknowledged. "Someday."

The steel-dust was trail weary and I traded him off for a good-looking, rangy buckskin. I wanted to be freshly mounted when I reached the Milk River country.

I hit Helena two days later. They were still digging gold out of Last Chance Gulch and the town was busting at the seams, with over seven thousand people. They were dancing in the streets, shooting and gambling day and night, gold changing hands quicker than fleas. It was too much for me, and I left before I could run into trouble, but not before I had seen nearly a thousand Long "D" cattle on sale there—the miners were too busy digging to game shoot, and the market was a big one, with beef prices sky high. I also learned the Blackfoot were kicking up some dust along the Marias, so I traveled with both eyes wide open, my Winchester across the saddle bow, keeping to the high ground and out of the breaks.

Twice I crossed sign—unshod ponies moving generally westward—and once found where the Blackfoot had made camp, but I saw no feathers until I hit Fort Benton, and it was Crow braves that were wearing them.

"You come to see your father?" someone asked as I tied up inside the fort. I turned, not liking the question, but when I saw a wily old Crow there I broke into a smile.

"Not exactly."

"The colonel's office is over there," he said.

"It has been a long time since we met that day. I was afraid. It seemed a good idea to tell you that my father was the commanding officer here. It wasn't until later that I found out you were from Fort Benton. Long ago . . ." I said, reminiscing.

"You were brave," the Crow said. "I remember how it was with the Gros Ventre. That Black Tooth!" He spit on the ground, spitting out the bitter taste of Black Tooth's name. "You have come home?" he asked.

"Yes. Home. But there are other whites who have taken my land."

"I feel sorrow for them," the Crow said, clasping my hand. "You were a brave boy. Now you are a man, a strong man."

It was a compliment I probably didn't deserve, but one I valued. For an Indian, any Indian, to tell you that you are a brave man is a tribute from a man who has lived his life in the raw of the wilds, fighting just to survive, living under a code which demands bravery from every member of the tribe.

I searched out the sutler's tent and bought a few

extra boxes of .44-40s for my rifle as well as the Colt which used the same cartridge, and a pound of coffee beans. I had a notion for a fine, narrow-bladed skinning knife I saw, but I was short on cash. Besides, I didn't know if I'd be doing any more hunting.

The sutler was a pleasant fellow and we stood talking about trail conditions, the Blackfoot, and about politics, of which I knew little. Behind me the door to the framed tent opened with the tinkle of a tiny bell.

"Got that flour, sutler?" the voice inquired and I stiffened at the sound of it. A kind of lisping, high-pitched voice, it was one I swore I'd never forget, and I hadn't. I turned to face the man named Bolen.

"Murdered anybody lately?" I asked quietly. He was looking at some combed cotton and his hands froze where they were. He looked up, not quite recognizing me. Then it must have hit him because his face twisted into a sickly smile and he began to sweat.

"I don't get you," he said.

"Don't you?" I was leaning against the counter, my elbows on it, staring at Bolen. He was a runner, Jake had told me once, but now I wasn't letting him run.

The sutler looked at Bolen and then at me and he backed away real easy.

"This man here," I told the sutler, "is one of them that shot down my father. Killed him cold for wages."

"Yule will . . ."

"Don't worry what Yule will do, Bolen. What will you do? I've got a hunch you'll do the same as Trollis and Free Wyler did—you'll die, Bolen."

"You don't know what the hell you're talking . . ."

He flagged it. Just as he went to draw his mouth went tight, his eyes narrowed, and he flinched. Then his pink hand dropped to the butt of his sidearm, but before it came up his face had gone slack, a purplish splotch soaking his shirt front. He shrugged and toppled forward, dead. A couple of soldiers broke into the tent, one of them with a rifle on me, but the sutler told it straight.

"Man tried to kill him. He was better."

Behind the soldiers was a crowd, the Crow among them. He grunted and turned away.

I left Fort Benton at dusk and nobody invited me back. I camped on a low knoll in sight of the fort and rolled up in my blanket, trusting to the horse and the proximity to the fort. At dawn I was already riding, my stomach filled with coffee and sourdough. I saw nothing the long day but a few head of shaggy buffalo and a magnificent bull elk. It was the following day when I caught sight of the south-bound trail herd.

Long "D" they were, and following the Marias, bound for the fort or possibly Helena. I sat in the shade of three lone oak on the rise and waited for them.

I caught them at their nooning. The cattle were drinking at the river with three hands to watch them while the others drank their coffee and had some beans and bacon. A couple of them were finished, patting their vests for the makings, talking in low voices. I came in easy, scanning their faces. They were cowhands, men who had drifted from Texas to Dodge and then come over to Colorado and hooked on with the Long "D" eventually. Honest, hard-working men they were, a few of them with thumbs missing from being too slow with that hitch around the pommel a cowhand has to make to slow a thousand-pound steer. And they were armed for bear . . . or Blackfoot.

Then I saw him and he saw me. His face twitched and he stood, smiling a toothless grin, his buckskins stained with years of use, his chin covered with a scruffy inch-long beard.

"Set," Jepitt said.

"I'm comfortable," I told Bake Jepitt, swinging my knee around the saddle horn, my rifle still across my lap.

"I always figgered you'd be back. I told Yule he was crazy to let you go. That's Yule, for you," Bake laughed. He laughed too long and then stopped suddenly, staring cold at me. "What do you want here?"

A few hands had come around my horse. Those who hadn't had their eyes on me, their hands free. They didn't know me and they didn't trust me. I figured I'd introduce myself.

"Name's Clay Rourke," I said, speaking up. And I went on to tell them what had happened between Yule DeLong and myself.

"And now you figger you got claim to these cows?" Bake Jepitt asked. His eyes shifted constantly, and I knew he was thinking the same thing I was—these cowboys rode for the brand, and were loyal to it. But they didn't know it was an outlaw brand.

"I don't hear you denyin' it, Jepitt," a tall, lazy-looking Texan said.

"I ain't denying it," Bake said sourly. "And you keep out of it Grich." He turned back to me. "Like I say—no matter how you figger it, these cows ain't yourn."

"No, but the grass in their bellies is. Suppose I start reclaiming that? Or you want to pay me for five years free graze?"

"You talk to DeLong—I reckon he'll settle up."

"I don't like the smell of this," Grich said. "I ride

for wages and work for 'em, if I say it my ownself. But I don't need wages this bad. I've ridden that grub line before, and I can do it again."

Grich and Jepitt had something between them, that I could see. Most of the others were just sitting and watching, seeing which way the wind blows. "I found Bolen," I said.

"So?"

"Had to kill him."

"Bolen couldn't shoot." Bake was stalling now, trying to move across my horse to the right side, the stock side of my rifle. He knew there was only one way out of this and so did I. When it came I still didn't expect it.

He pulled his pistol, but he was directly in front of my horse. He took the reins of the buckskin and jerked up hard. The buckskin shied and twisted away, and I had to grab leather. As I did Bake Jepitt shot. Three times in quick succession. At the crack of the first shot I pressed close to the buckskin and grabbed my own revolver. Bake's shot ticked off my saddle and whined off into the distance. The second was better, but my horse was moving for him as well as for me, and he was slightly off, the bullet cutting a chunk from my ear. The third shot hit nothing that I could tell, and by then I was to the ground, the horse stamping between us. Then I let him go off and we stood facing each other, Bake Jepitt and me, each of us with his gun in hand.

We touched off our shots. I aimed at the belt buckle and then stepped to the side slightly and aimed at the base of his neck. This one tore his throat open as his shot exploded in my ear, barely missing again. He was game, I'll give him that, and he eared back the hammer on his Colt with both thumbs and brought it up trembling as the blood from his throat flowed over his shirt and was soaked up by the dry earth.

He never got the muzzle up. I fired again and this one stopped his heart. He fell backward as if kicked by a mule, landing on his back, the pistol falling uselessly to the earth.

I stood there sweating, the dust sticking to me, the cool breeze stirring the trees, the sun hot in the high sky.

"There's eight of us," a stubby little man with a bulldog head said.

"Are you in it?" I asked, the Colt still warm in my hand. "There's no need for you to be. I've a couple more shots, mister. And you'd be the first."

"Hell, I've got no grudge against you, Rourke. Special as of what you said about DeLong and Jepitt killing your daddy. But I ain't like Grich there. I'm too old for that grub line, and I ain't been paid this month. You gonna pay us for what we done? I figger Yule DeLong is payin' us, and I'm working for him."

"You take these cows," I told him. "You sell them where you want—Helena or Fort Benton. Then divide up the money among yourselves. That'll give you six months wages easy."

"That's cattle stealin'."

"No, it's not. Not the way I look at it. These cows were dropped out of rustled stock from Colorado. If any of you been on the Long "D" for any time, you know the brands their mamas wore were a mixed batch. They been fed on my range, watered with my water. They don't belong to Yule DeLong, and I'm giving them to you. Besides, DeLong won't be in business after tomorrow. He won't be calling anybody thief."

"Suppose it don't work that way? I've seen the boss shoot."

"It might end that way. But I'd advise you to get shut of that outfit anyway. There'll be trouble sooner or later. If I'm killed there'll be another shooting one day—and you'll all likely be involved in it. DeLong is poison. If you haven't learned that yet, you will.

"You boys go on now. Sell those cows. And keep an ear open. If you hear DeLong is dead, come around. I might have work for a few of you. If you hear the other way—that I'm dead—then keep on ridin'. California is pretty country."

TWENTY-SIX

———◆———

My name is Clayborne Rourke. I came home to my ranch in the late summer of 1873, five years after I had left her green loveliness for the long trail over mountain and desert, on the seas, and in the pits called cities. I sat my buckskin pony on the hill I called Wagontongue for an old and splintered relic I had found there as a child of eleven, and I watched the smoke curling up from the ranch house chimney not fifty feet from where the old, burned-out house had been, the house my father had built with his sweat and muscles.

I sat there a long while, just remembering and watching. Then I rode down off that hill and finished what had been begun the day a cold-blooded killer and thief had decided it was easier to take what he wanted than to work for it as other men did. He must never have known the pleasure of watching things take shape and grow under his roughened hands, learning the satisfaction of doing things well, of resting when the day's work was done and the sun has cooled, and of knowing that what he built was built lasting and was worthwhile.

I rode down from the Wagontongue and went looking for that man.

There was only the one horse in front of the stone

house. It was a dirty-faced white with a hand-tooled saddle, with loosened cinch and no sign of sweat on him. It shook its head at me and stamped, but did not whinny as I tied the buckskin beside it and went up on the porch.

When I opened the door he was there. Sitting with his back to me in a big red-leather chair behind a waxed desk with a few papers in neat stacks.

"Rourke?" the voice was tired, old.

"Yes, it's me, DeLong."

"I always figured you'd come back."

"Then why didn't you kill me?" The room was dark, damp smelling, with only a dust-flecked stream of light from the far window, painting a swatch of yellow on the hard-packed floor.

"Why? Because I knew I could kill you whenever I had to if it came to that." He placed the finger of one hand to his temple and sighed just audibly. "I told you once long ago to learn your limitations and learn there is always someone who can go beyond them."

"But now, Yule, it's different. I'm quick, and you've gotten on in years. Your reflexes have slowed some."

"Yes," he admitted, "and so a man becomes more subtle." He swiveled suddenly in his chair to face me and I saw it on his lap—a nickel-plated Colt .44, like some tiny, beautiful, and deadly animal sleeping in his hand. DeLong's eyes were cold beneath his delicate, feminine lashes. His face was raw and haggard, lines cut deeply into it especially around the broad, sad mouth.

"You see?" he said. "I have you."

"I guess you do—only that won't stop me."

We were close together and locked in that stone-walled house. We were good shots, and even our misses, broken to fragments on the walls, would become deadly ricochets. There was no way either of us would walk from that room untouched.

"Well . . ." he shrugged nonchalantly, and some reflex within me was alerted. Somehow I knew that this was the beginning of his move.

A sheer fraction of a second before his thumb hooked the hammer of that fancy Colt my own hand swept up and the gun in it was erupting with flame and thunder.

A violent thrust knocked my knee from under me, and a wave of sharp pain tunneled into my brain. Following an instinct, I dropped to the floor and fired, my gun roaring like a prophet of doom. The room was thick with the rolling, acrid smell of gunpowder, and I saw Yule DeLong, firing from the hip, take a shot through the shoulder.

"Boy! Boy!" he shouted. I had come to my knees and we were looking into each other's eyes, and through, to the nerves that ran behind our eyes. Together we touched off our shots, the bullets passing each other in mid-flight. I was jerked halfway up and slammed against the wall behind me, the bellow of the shots still echoing in the stone room.

Grabbing the door latch, I pulled myself up, surprised that I could still do so. I was covered with a warm, sticky sensation, and my ears rang, my skin prickled with heat.

But Yule DeLong was down, sagged against the desk, his papers littering the floor near him, the nickel-plated Colt just beyond the reach of his twitching fingers.

"She sang good," he said through the choking blood in his throat. He coughed twice, his face going crimson, then flat white. "She danced and she sang, Clay. She was pretty to watch. She gave a fine performance. Though I can't say I care much for the finale . . ." He coughed again and arched his back with pain. I was trembling convulsively with the shock now, the numbing pain rising in my head, my stomach turned over with a violent sickness. I banged against the door, throwing it open, and I staggered out into the cool open air, the long blue sky washing away the smoke, the sickness—everything but the shattering pain. I took one more step, the gun dangling from my hand, and fell to the earth.

I heard a horse walking up, but I couldn't turn my head. I waited while the rider stepped from the creaking saddle and came up to me, while the lights of the day spun in a kaleidoscope of color and needles of pain inside my eyes.

"Howdy, you still hiring?" Grich asked.

He buried Yule DeLong out beyond the willows and put a marker on the spot. I was three weeks in that hard bed before I got tired of it and climbed on out one morning when the first frost had colored the grass and put a skin on the rain barrel.

Grich was repairing the woodshed, his mouth full of nails when he saw me. He grinned and climbed down, swaggering over to me.

"You don't look half bad," he said. I nodded, hanging on to the porch rail still as I got used to the blood circulating.

"New hand," Grich told me. He motioned with his head and I saw the Indian coming toward us, a post hole digger in his hand.

"Polecat . . . ? Polecat!"

"Clay," he smiled. "I came up last week. You look fine. The ranch too. Montana—everything looks fine."

"It does," I agreed. "How would you like it? You and Grich?"

Polecat was puzzled. He and Grich exchanged looks. "You all right in the head, Clay?"

"I'm all right."

"You're offering us the ranch? The ranch you fought for, dreamed of every night for five years?"

"Yes, I am. I did a lot of thinking in that bed. I'm going back to Colorado. I don't know what I'll do there, how things will work out. But there's a girl there who means more to me than all of this. Something I never got around to telling her—I guess I didn't know it myself. But now I do."

"You won't have the strength for a time yet," Grich said, removing his hat to scratch his head. He peered into the skies. "Weather's about to set in, looks like. It'll be a rough trail once the snows start. Besides," he added slyly, "Wendy would sure miss you."

"Wendy? Why, what . . . ?"

Then I turned to where they were looking, and I felt a flush crawl up my neck, and my heart started a thumping. Wendy was standing right behind me, a faint smile on her delicate lips.

"I did a lot of thinking too, Clay. About the kind of life I wanted. This should be our home. It's where we belong. Together."

She was wearing a buckskin skirt and a plain cotton blouse. Her hair was pulled back simply, and she wore no debutante's powder and no jewelry, but at that moment she was the most beautiful thing I had seen my life through. And partner, she still is.

DELL'S ACTION-PACKED WESTERNS

Selected Titles

Dell Bestsellers

- [ ] **TO LOVE AGAIN** by Danielle Steel $2.50 (18631-5)
- [ ] **SECOND GENERATION** by Howard Fast $2.75 (17892-4)
- [ ] **EVERGREEN** by Belva Plain $2.75 (13294-0)
- [ ] **AMERICAN CAESAR** by William Manchester . . . $3.50 (10413-0)
- [ ] **THERE SHOULD HAVE BEEN CASTLES**
  by Herman Raucher $2.75 (18500-9)
- [ ] **THE FAR ARENA** by Richard Ben Sapir $2.75 (12671-1)
- [ ] **THE SAVIOR** by Marvin Werlin and Mark Werlin . $2.75 (17748-0)
- [ ] **SUMMER'S END** by Danielle Steel $2.50 (18418-5)
- [ ] **SHARKY'S MACHINE** by William Diehl $2.50 (18292-1)
- [ ] **DOWNRIVER** by Peter Collier $2.75 (11830-1)
- [ ] **CRY FOR THE STRANGERS** by John Saul $2.50 (11869-7)
- [ ] **BITTER EDEN** by Sharon Salvato $2.75 (10771-7)
- [ ] **WILD TIMES** by Brian Garfield $2.50 (19457-1)
- [ ] **1407 BROADWAY** by Joel Gross $2.50 (12819-6)
- [ ] **A SPARROW FALLS** by Wilbur Smith $2.75 (17707-3)
- [ ] **FOR LOVE AND HONOR** by Antonia Van-Loon . . $2.50 (12574-X)
- [ ] **COLD IS THE SEA** by Edward L. Beach $2.50 (11045-9)
- [ ] **TROCADERO** by Leslie Waller $2.50 (18613-7)
- [ ] **THE BURNING LAND** by Emma Drummond $2.50 (10274-X)
- [ ] **HOUSE OF GOD** by Samuel Shem, M.D. $2.50 (13371-8)
- [ ] **SMALL TOWN** by Sloan Wilson $2.50 (17474-0)

At your local bookstore or use this handy coupon for ordering:

Dell **DELL BOOKS**
P.O. BOX 1000, PINEBROOK, N.J. 07058

Please send me the books I have checked above. I am enclosing $ _____
(please add 75¢ per copy to cover postage and handling). Send check or money
order—no cash or C.O.D.'s. Please allow up to 8 weeks for shipment.

Mr/Mrs/Miss _____

Address _____

City _____ State/Zip _____